W9-BWR-992

Ghost Soldiers

Steven Hardesty

Walker and Company
New York

c. 4

First published in the United States of America in 1986 by the
Walker Publishing Company, Inc.

Published simultaneously in Canada by John Wiley & Sons
Canada, Limited, Rexdale, Ontario.

Library of Congress Cataloging-in-Publication Data

Hardesty, Steven, 1946-
    Ghost soldiers.
    1. Vietnamese Conflict, 1961-1975—Fiction.
I. Title.
PS3558.A622G4   1986   813'.54   86-1320
ISBN 0-8027-0889-7

Printed in the United States of America

10 9 8 7 6 5 4 3 2 1

Part I

1

A company of American soldiers in
Vietnam rises from the dead to refight
a battle the way it should've been
fought.

PROTECTED BY INFANTRY, by guncars and helicopters,
truck convoys ground up the two asphalt lanes of Highway
19 and wound quickly through the hills of the Vietnamese
coastal province, away from the beaches and jungle heat,
up onto the cool plateau of the Central Highlands. The
convoys cut west through corn country, lettuce country,
bean country, across cool Deo Mang Pass and into the core
of Binh Dinh Province, into the city of An Khe under the
gaze of the jungle warriors of five armies. In An Khe the
convoys delivered rifles, rifles designed for American arm-
lengths and American finger-sizes, rifles intended for the
American soldiers squatting in their highland camps waiting
for the war to end. Then the relentless convoys ground on
over Bridge 25, into Mang Yang Pass, past the graves of a
thousand French legionnaires, and across the dusty plateau
carrying their rifles to other cities and other soldiers.

In the armories of the great American base at An Khe lay
new rifles, small, black M16 rifles; weapons that with the
flip of a switch could become light machine guns. The men
of the five armies—Yanks, Arvins, Koreans, Chucks and
North Viets—ignored these rifles as they ignored the mechanics of war that had brought them, living in their reveries of the war's imminent end. They were deceived; the
mechanics of war deceived them.

3

To the commanders of the American base camp it seemed pointless to continue issuing American rifles to American soldiers when the war, so nearly over, was intended to train and equip the South Vietnamese, so the new rifles were distributed to Arvin soldiers instead. These soldiers sold their rifles to the Chucks or to the Korean soldiers for seventy-five dollars apiece; their starving families needed the money. A few generous Koreans resold the rifles for two hundred dollars apiece to the American soldiers who were helpless without good rifles. Normal troop rotation caused most of these bought-back rifles to be sent with their Yank owners into the highlands forests and jungles, where the soldiers of five armies dreamed of the war's end. The rifles—the product of a simple mechanic of war—renewed the killing, and the war did not end.

Second Lieutenant W.A.L. Daugherty, 05-429-874, First Battalion, Second Field Artillery Regiment, was a Forward Observer (FO), a soldier who was never going to be issued an American rifle. The U.S. Army gave him one each: pistol, automatic, 45-caliber, and eight each: rounds, 45-caliber, and one each: magazine, 45-caliber. That was supposed to see him through the war and get him home alive.

His friends called him Waldo. To the men monitoring the Five Direction Control (FDC) radio net, he was call sign Yonkers two-four. He was a man of middling height and, before the war, of middling character. His head was remarkable only for the huge ears that stuck out on either side of a sunburned face made pale only by comparison to his clutch of wild hair black as asphalt.

If Waldo was asleep when the chopper went down, others were awake in that night, velvet black and thick as only a tropic night can be, with the smell of candles burning in the fog and Orion swinging in the sky above Old Baldy and its twin, Hill 415. A young and jittery soldier watching from a sandbagged bunker on lonely Bridge 25 was awake. He spotted the flashing red lights of a shot-up heli spinning down behind the saddleback, and reached for the landline.

Staff Sergeant Willard Mars also was awake, sitting at the NCO club bar. Sar'n Mars, with a drooping gray handlebar mustache and a perfect baldness that made his head look like a giant thumb, held curious prejudices for a soldier. He drank no coffee, ate no beef. He believed his enemies on the battlefields of the underdeveloped world were men starved of those commodities and so could smell them on his breath. Consequently, in the field Mars bathed rarely and only with antiviral soaps. He ate native foods and feasted only rarely on the muck served in army C ration cans. Nor did he sleep with his weapons. He was a light and restless sleeper with instant reflexes, and he dreaded that he might shoot a friendly if he were startled awake. More soldiers die by accident or by wounds inflicted by comrades than on the battlefield.

A tingling in the back of his skull, an instinct, told him the heli needed him, a death cry from machine to man; he froze at the NCO club bar like a man touched by God, his hands flung out across the bar to grasp the planed ammo-case wood, knocking glasses and Scotch to the cement floor. His fellow NCOs cursed him as they kicked the shards under the bar and shouted for more booze. Mars rose from his stool and went banging through the door, his company buck sergeants, Knobs and Georgie Bee, following him on the run, their jungle boots slapping the cement while the other NCOs stared.

Sar'n Mars stood in the open doorway of the cubicle in the officers' shack, walls of wood stripped from ammo crates and supported outside by rotting sandbags where rats ran. The radio played softly, and under his mosquito net Waldo slept the sleep of exhaustion. He was stark naked save for his dog tags and laced jungle boots; flesh slashed by elephant grass, nicked, bruised; his black hair flung out on the sweat-stained pillow; one hand spread across an infected wound on his chest, the other arm stretched out on the floor, the hand covered with his olive green bush hat. "Never seen a man sleep like that in base camp," said the black Sergeant Knobs, shifting from one march-sore foot to the other on his bowed legs.

Without entering the room, Mars stretched a hand toward the radio and slowly, evenly raised the volume. Waldo slowly and easily uncurled from under his netting, the bush hat falling from his hand, and he brought up to eye level the .45 pistol he had had there, his thumb clicking off the safety, the two bucks wide-eyed, Mars saying, "It's Sar'n Mars, Lieutenant, it's me," as Waldo's blue eyes cleared and he came conscious. He dropped the pistol to his bed, Knobs and blond, red-faced Georgie Bee, glanced at each other, the glance saying, "This one's crazier'n the rest of us."

"Chopper down," said Mars. Waldo nodded: Of course! You finally pull three days' R and R after weeks of humping in the field and some bastard takes a fall. Of course, of course! He dressed, slung his artillery net radio over his shoulder, the .45 on his hip, the pack of C rats on his back, the compass on its shoestring at his neck, rubbing his hand over the sweat-glistening combat shave on his cheeks. There would be no shave, no shower. It was all as though he'd never waked or never slept; his choices only waking nightmare or the sleep of the dead.

When Reginald "Peepsite" Taylor thought about it, which was something he rarely did (soldiers can afford to think about nothing but war or they will die, he was convinced), he believed that if he wasn't really there, they couldn't really kill him. It was a brilliant solution to the problem of how to survive the war. A good deal of the time he dreamed of himself in college—as a high-school dropout, college was his great ambition—in a vast blue lecture hall crammed with eager fellow students, many more jamming the doors, listening to a fantastic college-type lecture on the mating habits of white rats or the history of quick-frozen orange juice. For hours he would be content and safe in that lecture hall. Then the war would intrude and he would remind himself and everyone around him that he wasn't really there.

Peepsite was not entirely satisfied with his solution as there were certain people—particularly the captain—who were prejudiced against it, and they were preventing him from making corporal. "Come back down to earth, Peeps," the captain would say, slapping Peepsite on the rump so hard Peeps spit out the bennies he was about to swallow. "Ya gotta cope, boy, ya gotta cope without them pills." Captain Oliver Foley was black. He'd wiggle his big brows above the thick glasses held onto his face with a strap around his head under his bush hat and clop up the trail, adjusting his pack straps and shaking his big Missouri ass. "Are ya copin, boy?"

When Mars, Waldo, and the bucks found Peepsite, he was sprawled on an endless, imaginary green lawn covered with pines and ivied buildings, feeling up a coed excited by his massive blackness, by his twisted nose and uneven eyes which gave the impression he was made of the two halves of two different men indifferently glued together.

"Chopper down, Peepsite," said Sar'n Mars.

"I ain't really here," Peepsite protested.

"I know, yeah. Let's go."

Captain Foley met them as he banged out the door of the dolly shack, his gear and weapons hanging from him in disarray. "Sar'n Mars, rouse the boys. Chopper down—just got the call from higher." He buckled his black gloves and they ran for the track park, men leaping from shadow, strapping on gear, slamming home mags, the armored personnel carriers grumbling like Mack trucks and spitting smoke, their gunners hooting for Bravo. Bravo Company, Captain Oliver Foley's company, forty-two men, a third of what was demanded in the field manuals, but this was Vietnam and no outfit was full strength. Then, neither was the enemy. Only the choppers and Sar'n Mars had all their magic in this war.

"Climb aboard—no time—chopper down!"

They crawled up the square sides of the aluminum boxes, pulling themselves up on the gunshields and grabbing the equipment tie-downs or bracing themselves against the .50 turret or the .30 machine-gun shields. The tracks clacked forward out of the park (flashing their Red Elephant logos and their Dixie battleflags) down the asphalt road laid between fields of weed toward the glaring watchtower lights of the main gate. They jerked hard right, piling on speed, the cowboys howling into the wind, Waldo's track leading them and Mars in mystical communion with the fallen chopper; they roared down the highway into Chuckie's jungle and the pouring rain, the tracks bouncing over ruts and gullies, the GIs clinging to the machine guns and their terror building to rage as they whistled and chanted, "Chopper down! Chopper down!" sliding over the wet decks, antennas and pennants flapping overhead.

They crashed into VC Valley at forty miles an hour firing flares into the fields around the sandbag bunker where stood the boy who had seen the chopper fall. They howled for entry onto Bridge 25, firing wildly with all guns into the dripping head-high elephant grass, streaks of good American orange tracer sizzling through Chuck's territory (the night) and slicing up Chuck's fog that sagged down the mountainsides. The young soldier who had seen the chopper fall swung back the wire barricade, pointed to the saddle between the two tree-covered mountains and said, "There!"

Mars and Captain Daddy shouted the Bravos into the elephant grass where each couldn't see the man next to him and with Waldo they swept south, platoons-on-line, bucking back the tall, wet weed with their rifle stocks as they left behind the comfort of the tracks' big guns.

The captain and Fruitcake took the point. Fruitcake was a natural for it—he was an acne-pitted, gangly country boy with the deliberate grace of a long-legged spider and he could smell bad gooks. He was also a coward who knew that no bushwhackers would risk alerting the company by blasting the point man, if they could help it, so despite his size he figured to survive the war. He also had dreams of winning a Bronze Star to go with his Combat Infantryman's Badge to show off back on the block, even though he knew only officers got the BS. He might get it if he were dead, of course, and that presented him a problem.

As for Captain Foley—he took the point because it was his fantasy that he was a soldier when he was really a Missouri village parson. The army had proved a delightful surprise to him. In Missouri he was considered a woods-man barely competent to find his way out of a parking lot. The army, however, was less demanding and cared not at all that he had once put his company on the wrong moun-taintop when the army sent choppers to pull them out of Chuck's pincers—the army just sent the choppers from the right mountain to the wrong mountain and got them out anyway, and gave him a BS for bringing back forty-two living bods and six wounded-in-action (WIA), none killed. That was an achievement: He won no battles but he got no one killed. Who won battles, Foley wondered? No one, really. What was a battle? You stumble through the jungle or the pine forest, half-blind from bennies, from exhaus-tion, from too much patrolling or fright or sweat or rain or sun, and you find yourself standing in a mess of surprised Chucks and you shoot them and they shoot you and you stumble away dragging your wounded thinking, God, we skirted the pit one more time, and then you stumble into another nest of Chucks and it goes on and on. No one at higher cares that your men are exhausted, war-weary, too frightened to blow grass, too frightened to carry bourbon in their canteens like Sar'n Mars. The helis never come on time or when they do they mistake you for Chuck and shoot you up. You never have enough to eat. You shoot up your ammo and *then* Chuck wants to fight you. You stink. Your boots are torn on pungi stakes. Diarrhea runs down your legs. The leeches eat you at night. No water. The men fall out by the trail in shivering exhaustion and you take them in your arms. You search for their salt tabs but their canteens are empty. When the whole mix gets too much for them they go nuts and throw tear gas grenades at one another, laughing like idiots. No one at higher gives a damn. The battalion commander (Batco) leaves in two weeks; he wants to go out in a blaze of glory and he really wants that Legion of Honor to pin on his chest, but he's never been out in the field (one of the lucky ones who got too old, too fat, too much rank between wars to have to fight in this one).

Dead French legionnaires pricked at the corners of his eyes. Foley turned to stare. They were gone in muted *pops!*, their strange grim smiles lingering. "I'm a rat that's jumped too often," he said aloud.

Loping Fruitcake looked at his captain in surprise, then cursed him softly. He was concentrating on his hands and feet—dreaming he hadn't any. He was trying to decide which he could do without to win his BS.

Waldo dropped out of a tree. He might as well have been out of the sky, he startled Fruitcake so badly. Fruitcake cursed again, louder, his reverie of sidewalk glory broken. He sulked ahead through the dripping weed, picking at his pimples, rain draining off his bush hat.

"Can't see any chopper flames nor a burn zone, Captain." Waldo clutched his radio mike. "Let me drop some flares. At least they'll know we're out here looking for them."

"Do that. Drop flares. The boy at the bridge had any idea how far behind that mountain it was when he saw it fall?"

"Naw, he's a stupid grunt. Yonkers three-one, three-one, this two-four, flare mission, over," Waldo said into his hand phone.

Waldo's battalion Fire Direction Control Center was in the middle of the battalion area in base camp, the camp's best-fortified above-ground bunker. Concrete foundations and a concrete slab floor supported six-by-six uprights keeping four layers of plastic-woven sandbags in neat military order for a roof. The inner walls were reinforced with perforated steel planking, the same used to cover the Golfcourse—the base-camp airstrip—and that hung with plywood for the huge plastic-sheathed maps that covered the walls. The portholes were heavily shuttered and the overhead cover three feet thick. In that immense heap of organized sand was a small, dark hole filled almost completely with a plotting table of plywood on sawhorses made from wood scrounged from ammo crates. Bare bulbs hung overhead. Radios stood against the wall. The computers worked with pencil and rule at their plotting boards in a suffocating, dank, dusty, dark atmosphere, sand dripping from the ceilings when enemy mortar rounds ranged over the bunker, old burger wrappers from the Airborne Club strewn on the rickety metal chairs.

The radio telephone operator (RTO) on duty relayed Waldo's commands to the base-camp guns, six dirty brown 105s with the power to burst eardrums with their roar, the gunbunnies opening the breeches between their trails for the projos to be rammed home. *WHAM WHAM WHAM!* and the hundred-pound rounds of steel and powder were sizzling overhead beyond the two green mountains and there, there! in the black filling with gray fog the flares burst, one after the other, in neat timed order so that there was always light, the flares sinking through the clouds on their parachutes flaming pink like angels descending into man's dangerous world. "Good," Waldo said into the mike, "good," and he tramped forward through the brush following Fruitcake, speaking softly into his hand phone adjusting the flares.

Captain Foley heard the whispered words, "Mikes comin' through," and got off the trail with Bravo, blinking his magnified eyes behind his thick lenses, his brows bobbing up and down. He dropped the utility strap from his shoulder and let his 16 rest there across his hip, aimed at the trail, the safety off and his finger on the trigger. The point man for the Viet militia company, the Mikes, came through the brush grinning like an idiot, fright in his eyes, his bush hat wrapped with his blue Mike scarf and his own fresh bright new M16 in his hands. He waved at Foley and trudged uptrail following the route Fruitcake had cut. Fruitcake was up there, having heard the whispers even where he was, crouching by the side of the trail with his rifle on go-go, waiting. The lead element came up, the Mike captain a martinet hissing commands at men too miserable in the cold rain to hear, fright in their eyes: What were they doing out after dark, risking their lives for a Yank chopper down? To hell with the round-eyes and their filthy war! Don't they know the dead crawl around up here at night? The Mike company went up the trail giggling nervously, passing cigs, waving their flashlights around.

The Bravos closed up trail behind them cursing. "Fruitcake," said Foley, "follow those bastards so long as they're headin' south into the valley. If they don't, you cut trail and keep us away from them."

"Yeah, Daddy." Fruitcake loped off into the fog swirling behind the last of the Mikes, the Mike with huge startled eyes gazing back at him.

Georgie Bee, brown-eyed, blond, red-faced, even after six months in Vietnam his skin still bubbling with scores of tiny water blisters, was sergeant of the First Platoon and took his plat's lead behind the company lead. Company lead was the captain, his RTO and one gunman, the best: Enrique "B-2" Saavedra. B-2 was a natural cowpoke, range-scrawny and with a Latin vanity that forced him to shave even in the jungle. He had huge, pale, wet, nervous eyes in worried sacks of black bagging on his olive cheeks. B-2 had come to them from the mechanized infantry where he'd survived a rocket through the side of his track—he was sitting on top, of course, and he was blown off and walked away from the wreck laughing in fright, and walked away from the mech because it was unsafe and his luck was up; a man can take one B-40 plastique shaped charge through his track and laugh out of his chattering teeth, but he'll never go back to the boxes and try it again, not if he's sane. Sar'n Mars was usually part of company lead, but now he was back with the tail, watching for Chucks creeping up on them; where the Mikes went, Chuck was sure to follow.

Now isn't that strange? thought the Bee. Georgie Bee was not a risk-taking man but he did believe in taking advantage of the ridiculous enthusiasms of others. Which is why he liked marching behind the captain. He followed exactly in Daddy's big footprints. No .30 bullet planted along the trail on top of a nail was going to blow a hole through his foot. If anyone was going to trip a mine or a jump-up grenade, let it be Daddy: that'd give the Bee time to hit the deck.

He led his platoon into the misty grass, the rain not slackening, ahead of them in the saddle of the two mountains the angel flares coming down, the ground underfoot oozing slime. The trees around them were leafless; the Bee would have thought of autumn had he not known the helis had defoliated this area. They crossed three tiny streams; water sloshed in his jungle boots and ran out the drain holes. It was cold; his teeth chattered. The air smelled like old socks. For a moment he shut out the sounds of the men around him and listened only to the jungle sounds—water

dripping, weed breaking in the wind, small animals frightened from their holes by the tramping feet, somewhere
under the lid of night a brushbuck barked.

Shouldn't be out in the rain, little brother, thought the
Bee. It was as though he was the first man ever to set foot
here on this slope, the ground so new and rich he could
almost believe his fantasy. He thought: If I stop for a
moment here in the black rain around this bend of trail, I'll
be alone. He thought: Do it now! Step left off the trail and
be alone. Be free. Disappear. *Go home!* He thought: Vietnam is a place a man can live the whole of his life under
skies as intense as cymbals' crashing, with dirt roads hot
through the soles of your boots, palms and pines of green-
yellow and silver, birches by the road, red jungle birds
cawing through the sky over stream-cut mountains, air that
smells and tastes fresh, a land filled with races of tigers and
men and women frightening and exciting.

It was a place where everyone he knew died. Where
some few he didn't know crawled home alive. What did it
mean to be a soldier in that place? This is what it meant: No
one was kind to him. There was no woman to give him a
soft word; the women there gave him Cokes filled with
battery acid or ground glass or they raised little naked
children who held pin-pulled grenades behind their backs.
He was hated at home as well. For the first time in his life
he was hated by people who knew him and by people who
didn't know him. That thought struck him with a cold and
bitter terror. He could not imagine that young man he had
once thought himself to be, a young man of crew-cut blond
hair, occupied with roaring cars, laughing girls burnt brown
in the Colorado sun, reckless pranks, and strange untested
ideas about good and evil. He had never suspected those
ideas would count for anything; now he wished he had
never heard of the war, that he might have gone his whole
life without testing those ideas. The boy who had been
himself lived a safer, cleaner, saner life, a more thoughtless

life, a life without test and strain; he was not the man who was here now slogging this jungle trail dragging his pack and rifle a thousand meters south into the valley—and tomorrow it would be a thousand meters west toward Pleiku or a thousand meters east toward the China Sea. But he had the chance to quit right here. Step off the trail and the war was finished.

At the bend he stepped offtrail and pushed into the brush. He squatted there watching the company pass, laughing to himself at how easily he had escaped the war. His body shook with his silent laughter and the chill rain. It was over. All over. He had been poor and ragged and ashamed and suddenly it was over! He had stepped out of life. He put the muzzle of his 16 into his mouth, put his finger on the wet trigger, and pressed. The firing pin thunked into the round and nothing happened. "My 16 doesn't misfire!" he wanted to shout. "Not *my* 16!" But it had. It was a sign: He was not going to die in Vietnam! That certainty put him beyond the power of strangers' hate, and he could do his soldier's job.

He ejected the bad round, broke it apart to deny it to Chuck, chambered another, and climbed out of the brush onto the trail where Sar'n Mars, the last man in the column, stood staring at him. Mars grabbed him by the collar and shoved him uptrail with a kick in the rump and on they went in their endless plodding shambling into the Valley.

From Mars at the tail of the column to Fruitcake on the point lost in the fog and elephant grass ahead, every man in the column was drifting through his own private reverie. It was a column of ghost soldiers marching through Chuckie's dangerous country, dreaming that the war would end. They had forgotten their mission—the helicopter—in their hard slogging through the mud and rain, climbing the mountainside, the stink of gook cigarette coming back to them from the Mikes ahead, and the Mikes, terrified in the dark, flashing their lights around the mountainside either to warn off Chucks or to frighten them or to make the Yanks targets of Chuckie's mortars, all that irritating the GIs. But nothing irritated them enough to break them free of their dreams, the dreams that saved them from the bleeding pack sores on their shoulders and rumps and the wet coldness in their stumbling wood feet. There were no bennies tonight to ease the pain. No one ate bennies in Chuck's night. The bourbon in Mars's canteen was untasted. There is no point in a soldier's thinking on his mission once he has decided to see it through.

Mars had spent this day in the war as he had spent so many days—all of the days—of his four years there, living without thinking about living, living with all thoughts covered because some part of his mind was traitor to the other part. In war a soldier cannot think beyond the moment or he will die. Back in Burgerland his wife and kids can be sprawled on the beach slurping ice-cream cones and so pass a long, lazy day thinking they've done well to spend their time so easily; but their soldier father-husband half a world away has lived a dozen lifetimes in their one beach day: A soldier gains or loses one life each time he grovels in the mud, hiding shrieking from enemy steel. Some soldiers, such as B-2, win lives now and then, and carefully husband what they've won. Others, and Mars was always one of the others, lose one life in each fight. How many lives had he to lose? Only Mars could say, and only he would know it when the last life was yanked away from him and he stood there naked to the enemy. Mars had no *family,* though he had a wife and three children he had not seen twice in four years. The army offered him home leaves and sometimes he took them at home and sometimes in Australian whorehouses. Was it the war or fear of his wife that made him stay four years in Vietnam when rational men were happy to go home whole after one? He preferred to think it was the war.

It was a morbid night and his mind crowded with morbid thoughts of the future. Some nights here smelled of clover and others of walnuts. He loved the days especially when the air was pale, light, and unburdened. Evenings, clouds would pillow on Hong Kong Mountain, sinking over base camp and the tough grass would crinkle under his boots as he walked through the camp with its tang of diesel and urine from the johns. The camp was filled with five thousand soldiers only five hundred of whom ever left the camp for combat; the rest passed their days counting bubblegum at the PX.

Mars was not a born soldier. Few men are. He was made a soldier. After an unremarkable but cold six months in the Korean conflict, in which he drew first blood on the enemy he always seemed to be fighting, and after eight years in a Stateside army post peeling spuds and wishing he were somewhere else, after a boost to corporal (and those were the grand old days when there were corporals in the army; now the wartime army was full of "Specialists" this class and that, but Specialists in what?)—he had the two gold chevrons sewn on his sleeves and was proud of them. He was made an acting sergeant, too, and that could have been made permanent with some hard work and good reports. But he did a soldierly thing and took an Irish buck sergeant into the coal room and beat him silly for the sake of a woman. The buck pulled a bayonet he had planted in the coal and Mars barely had the presence of mind to kick the buck in the head, ending the fight without bloodshed. The sergeant wobbled a bit when Mars put him on his feet and booted him homeward, but he was okay. The bayonet went into the furnace. It wasn't the fight that cost him his two new stripes, it was the bayonet in the furnace. He'd wasted U.S. government property. The Irish top sergeant was decent about it. No Article 15 before the captain, just no stripes, and out of the company into the Rathole, the holding company where the regiment kept its misfits—the fags, the degenerates, and the Georgia-clowns who figured they could get out of their draft time by beating up junior officers. They were all waiting their time to collect their Dishonorables and that train ticket home. He hated the Rathole; he was a soldier and proud of it, though he had been nothing but a potato-peeling career private up to then. There was one way out of the holding company and that was Vietnam. After Korea war didn't frighten him. He volunteered. The army was glad to have him in the quota; it meant one fewer draftee to worry about.

Everything about Vietnam was strange to him and nothing was anything like what they'd told him to expect. They'd dropped him on the China Sea coast and he'd tramped around a sort of jungly desert that later was called the Street Without Joy, but the Fiftieth Mech, the Sixtyninth Armored, and the Seventeenth Artillery knew it as the Bong Son Plain, a place where every tree harbored a Chuck. They were good smart Chucks, who set traps for tanks and blew them away, who set traps for grunts and blew them away, who set traps for the guns and blew them away. And there was nothing to save the Yanks but the Hawkeyes, a half dozen pilots in little Birddogs who would go up and get crazy at all the Chucks they'd see. When they'd call down the ambushes they'd sighted, the Batcos would ignore them and send in the tanks and the grunts World War II style. But they weren't fighting the Nazis or the Japs. They were fighting Chuckie in another dimension of warfare and they couldn't get at him. But he could get at them. It was unfair that the U.S. Army was that stupid.

What saved PFC Willard Mars was the battleship *New Jersey*. She skulked off the coast, and when the Hawkeyes or the ground FOs called in her fire, Mars thought, Who needs nukes or the air force if ya got the *Jersey?* He had thought eight-inch howitzers punching out their hundred-and-fifty-pound shells could tear up a piece of real estate, but when that lady off the coast turned her guns on Vietnam, there was no Vietnam left. She loved to run range and

deflection spreads or rolling fires that plowed up and
plowed up and plowed up the land, flashing all over orange
and black, chunks of steel the size of Volkswagens singing
crashing overhead. Old Chuckie didn't like that lady; she
came after him from another world and it was a world he
couldn't touch.

The Sixty-ninth Armored was a skull-taking outfit; they
paraded into battle with Chuck heads bleeding on their
tanks. That magic did them no good; they were still torn to
pieces. And Mars was among them. His second week in the
war and nothing was as it was supposed to be, nothing but
the lady. He rode into battle with his shining bald head
camouflaged under a bush hat and with two weeks' Nam
experience. Already he had had his second Combat Infantryman's Badge for his dress greens, proving that he had
stepped before the fire in two wars and had lived. He didn't
want any of the other badges, the Purple Puke or the BS,
because he had already seen what a man had to pay to get
them. In they went holding the rear of the tank turrets and
standing over the grates pumping hot air from the tank
engines, the mech infantry tracks streaming alongside with
all their GIs sitting on top of the boxes. He was with a navy
corpsman from the *Jersey,* some fool who thought he could
get himself a CIB and volunteered to hump the radio for the
arty FO who was there with Mars, too.

It was a good fight. It lasted thirty seconds, and Chuck
was happy with the results. A platoon each of mech and
armor was wiped out; it was fog or smoke from the *Jersey*'s
fire that clouded the field and saved Mars's life. He lolled
back along his poncho, pulled it over his bleeding bald head
and turned his face against the ground. Babies cried. Phantoms slithered past. Purple mists shifted densely around his
face. Odors of sweat and rotting alien things trembled in the
fog. He began to sob over his shattered M16. Silence! His
ears twisted and sucked. Were they coming? Was he the
only one left alive? Emptiness! His body began to stiffen at

the joints and he thought he was dying. Better to die now in this quiet peace than let Chuckie take him. He turned slowly, curling into a comma, the muscles of his throat pulling his lips from his teeth; he could feel himself take on the appearance of a dead man. So he was dying. Thank God!

He couldn't feel his hands or feet. He ground his face into the earth, whimpering. Along his side only the oozing wound was animate. He made himself a lump of ground, waiting for the half moon of night to brush his camouflage poncho and hide him. With evening or dawning, he didn't know which, he began to disappear. Tigers passed him and fed on the corpses of others. Cobras holding their hoods waist-high slicked over his plastic sheet trailing sweet-smelling slime. A single water buffalo dunged on the stubs of his legs. Only his tears remained material. Where were the choppers? Why hadn't the army cleared this field? He rolled open one eye and watched as masses of fog cartwheeled around the clearing, carving back the jungle and leaving nothing but Chuck faces staring at him from the trees, phantoms that came toward him, and he screamed but his tongue had disappeared. Their tentacles plucked away his uniform. Their flesh was cold and rough. The tallest nudged him over on his back, grunted, and turned to walk away.

Mars's body came alive: "Help me! Help me!" he cried. The fog burst apart; blue sky rushed into the clearing. "Not catatonic after all," said the tallest GI. "You can get up now, buddy." "No, he can't. Look at that hole in his side." "Christ, what a mess! Thought he was a shirker or a coward. Help him up, you two." The tall one, the NCO, detailed two men to help drag Mars along. There was no time for a medevac chopper and the field was still hot, so they had to run for it. The fight had lasted thirty seconds and Mars had been there in his delirium five minutes more before they had found him. He staggered toward the jungle between his rescuers' arms and found the navy corpsman's brainless head, eyes sunk back, the great pink cavity lined with veins. He dipped his fist into its emptiness, searching for whatever silver threads there are that make men men. In that moment he believed he saw that there is no mystery to life: We are all animals and no one survives.

2

ON THE BRAVOS staggered, uphill, some of them thinking dimly about the downed helicopter and wondering if they would find survivors. Had the chopper fried them? Had Chuck vivisected them? It was all the same to the skinny, worried-eyed, Latin cowboy B-2, slogging along there behind Captain Daddy, a post he had assumed for himself because the captain was such a clumsy oaf everyone knew he'd let himself be blown away if Enrique Saavedra weren't there to bodyguard him. B-2 was part of a different war. His war had all the dreariness and confusion of all the other wars being fought that night on the mountainside, but his war was a war with Purpose: Vietnam was going to make him rich.

To the forty-one others in Bravo Company (plus Waldo the FO who was not a grunt but attached to them from the redleg battalion), B-2 was an old-fashioned berserker, something belonging on a Viking ship or with Duke William storming up Hastings Hill to cross sword and ax with King Harold. General Custer could have used him. He stood in his fights like a madman, spraying the enemy—for him the enemy seemed hill, tree, stone, as well as men—and putting his bullets and his body between his buddies and death. B-2 knew he should not be alive now; he had taken too many stupid chances. But he thought he would survive this war,

23

unlike most of the others who accepted the terrifying
statistics. Only one in twelve U.S. soldiers actually fought.
Of the infantry, each combat soldier would be wounded
once, each officer twice, fate determining which was fatal
and which was not. B-2 would survive because he had
Purpose. It had been a long dirty day months ago that had
led to the moment that gave him Purpose.

B-2 had been in the mechanized infantry then.
Dirty Dave, a lieutenant who was something of a
dandy—a tall, clean-skinned, yellow black with his fruity
little mustache and his stupid red beret ("Let him wear that
idiot thing," his plat would say. "Let him attract the steel,
keep it away from us.")—led them through bright, boring
days, crashing through the boonies, knocking down trees
with their tracks, plinking at tin cans with their stolen .45s,
chopping off branches with machine-gun fire, and getting
the boxes stuck in the mud. Armored personnel carriers
bog down easily when they fight in the wrong terrain in the
wrong war, and they throw track just bumping into trees.
With two platoons—eight tracks—and their commanding
officer along for the ride and Dirty Dave's box in the lead,
they had to stop for four mechanical failures and seven
stickings in the thigh-deep mud. They spent six hours in the
hill country, traveling four miles total on the tops of those
hot, hard boxes, getting stiff, skin peeling, those foolish
too-heavy-to-wear helmets on their heads (they wore them
that day to satisfy the CO who hated them, too, but had to
please the Batco who never left his battalion area in base
camp, his beer, and his burgers). Branches slapped their
faces. Fat black and yellow spiders dropped from the
bamboo and scampered over them. The water simmered in
their canteens. Sunbaked. Dust-grease-sweat. The constant
breakdowns. After a full morning of that nonsense the
mech infantry forgot about looking for Chucks and started

looking for an easy route home, tracing it on the FO's map. They found a booby trap and some old foxholes and blew them; that provided some diversion. But no enemy. All through this frustrating, typical day the CO cracked jokes and diddled his mustache and stood in the thickest mud working on the stuck tracks. The man was imperturbable; he irritated them endlessly. They didn't realize that this outing away from the Batco was a lark for the CO, like a boy let out of school by surprise.

Vietnam was a war of military intelligence, or so the senior officers believed. They also believed that good "intel" was more important than good soldiering. And a day studying maps and photos in base camp was a day closer to rotation home and a safer day than prowling the woods with the grunts. If the soldiering couldn't achieve the results the intel promised, the reports to higher simply needed a little more creative writing than usual. Every level had its intel and every level had its reports. A field body count of two KIA and two WIA VC-suspect always became six KIA and twenty WIA confirmed VC/NVA at battalion level. Batt justified it simply. You could never count on those stupid grunts to have the guts to actually go poking through those booby-trapped woods to collect all the meat after a firefight, so a certain additional number had to be added for accuracy's sake—and if arty was used then that meant some bods just got atomized or blown up into treetops, so another percentage had to be counted in. As the report climbed the ladder to brigade and division and corps and to the commanding general's desk, it grew from that original two and two to twenty killed and a hundred wounded VC/NVA/Laotians. What struck the GIs in the field as odd about the system was that the general actually seemed to believe the reports he was fed, even though he had done the same type of "reporting" himself in the last war he'd fought. While the intel reports going up the chain were inflated and believed, intel coming down the chain was reported scrupulously and just as scrupulously disbelieved by the GIs in the field.

The morning of the day that B-2 found Purpose, the CO had gotten official word to expect a "general uprising" through Two Corps Tactical Zone at exactly 0900. He ignored it. Just at the moment their first track bogged down in mud in Chuckie's wild woods, the enemy hit Landing Zone (LZ) Action with its fire base of six howitzers, and hit pump station Number 3 on this side of the Mang Yang, using mortars and recoilless rifles. The CO followed the action around their Area of Operations on his blue net radio; it was like watching TV—a lot of fun and no pain for him. Then the Hawkeyes in their little spotter planes reported two plats VC and later a company of eighty men in blue and gray uniforms with .30 machine guns and 82mm mortars. That was serious news. But they intermingled with civilian woodcutters and the arty couldn't shoot them and they vanished. Mike Force, the Vietnamese highly irregular militia, skirmished in the southwest with the VC. A Ruffpuff home guard day ambush made a minor contact and then overran a VC-prone village and pulled some Ak47 automatic rifles and rocket-propelled grenades from the village well. That was the high point of the general uprising and a typical day in the highlands where the five armies staring eyeball to eyeball really had no interest in fighting so long as things stayed as they were. After all, the war was about to end. What made the day unusual was the money.

Dirty Dave was bored with whining around while the CO and the others tried to pry the command and control track out of the mud, so the CO told him to recon the surrounding hills and Dave, adjusting his red beret and dabbing a little mud on the shine of his yellow black cheeks, led out before his plat had time to form up. They trailed after him. Away from the mud, the flies, the sweat, the army was a lark again, and they were hunting. They had humped an hour into the hills before the pleasure of their freedom had begun to wear and their minds had turned to thoughts of chow when B-2 saw him—one gook running like hell through the brush—and saved them all from boredom. The tree cover wasn't thick enough to worry a mortar round, so Dirty Dave walked fire from the 60mm mortar—a tube the size of the tube that comes in a roll of kitchen towels—and they dropped steel on the gook, howling, "Busted his ass, right on, hey!" and then scrambled after the enemy to see what he had in his pack to split up for the spoils of war.

The bloodtrail stopped in the grass. It was as though the gook had jumped up into the sky and disappeared. "Spider hole, gotta be a spider hole round here," said Dave, drawing his bayonet and digging in the earth looking for the hidden entrance. "Get some frags ready. B-2, stand by to blast him if he pops up in my face."

"We really shouldn't do this, Lieutenant," said Saavedra, looking around uneasily from the great bruised sacks of worry in which his eyes sat, looking at the plat streaming from the woods and bunching around the spider hole. "They've likely got covering MGs in other holes."

"Naw, this guy was just an observer for 'em. There!" Dave slid his bayonet under the lip of the hole's lid and swung up the false covering of sod and matting on a tunnel gleaming with blood. There was no one to be seen in it. "Flashlight," he called. He started to climb in.

"Could be booby-trapped, Lieutenant," said B-2.

"Frag it then, worrywart," ordered Dave. They threw in grenades. Then Dave climbed into the blood-slimy hole, motioning B-2 to follow. "Can't be too deep for only one guy. Where's the RTO? Bring the radio just in case."

The radioman hesitated. "Radio won't do you much good down there, Lieutenant."

"Come on, come on!"

The RTO followed and thus saved his life. Just as he went

into the hole, the last of the platoon streamed out of the trees and stood there gawking into the pit—and the enemy's covering machine guns opened fire. The three of them— B-2, Dirty Dave, and the RTO—tumbled deep into the pit, smearing themselves with the gook's blood, and found themselves at the conjunction of three tunnels weakly lit by candles.

"Good God," whispered the RTO, "this ain't no spider hole. This's a regimental CP!" They stared at each other with huge eyes as the machine gun firing racketed over- head—and the screams.

"What do we do now?" said B-2.

Dirty Dave adjusted his red beret and said, "Keep fol- lowing the blood trail and hope we ᴜᴜd an exit through another spider hole, then we run like mad."

They went crouching through the low, narrow tunnels following the blood and found the corpse heaped on a platform carved from the earth—a bed, perhaps—in a tunnel that was slightly larger and equipped like a squad bay with bedrolls, rucksacks, cooking stoves vented through shafts to the forest floor above. They found one more squad bay and that was it, plus the strongbox. It was a U.S. Army footlocker painted with gook symbols. Who- ever had been interrupted in doing the tally sheets that lay strewn in the dirt around it had improperly secured the lock. Like good GIs always alert for souvenirs, Dave pulled off the lock and they flung open the trunk. They would have snatched a little something of what was inside—a brass NVA belt buckle with the star on it or a gook flag—and then followed Dave's plan to run for the first exit and safety, but the thing was full of bright crisp U.S. green Burgerland dollars. And lots of the Fu Manchu stuff the Arvins used. "Must be a million or more!" said Dave, grabbing up a pack of hundreds.

"Got to be counterfeit," said B-2. "Forget it. Let's go."

"No, no, no," said the RTO, mesmerized, laying his

hands on the money as though in prayer. "This is a Chuck paymaster station and this is *real*. They don't pay their boys counterfeit." With that they dived into it, stuffing their pockets and packs.

"We'll get out to tell the others," said Dave. "But this can't get back to batt."

"Whadya mean? This is spoils of war. They can't take it from us," said B-2.

"U.S. Army don't take spoils," said the RTO. "That's in the regs."

"We keep our mouths shut." Dave led out, greed investing him with a new and unaccustomed fury. He and B-2 went up the last tunnel together like two berserkers, the RTO hanging back in fright, firing their 16s go-go and sweeping the tunnel clean, clambering over four bods and a wrecked MG and throwing off the spider hole lid shouting to the others in the plat as Dave and B-2 opened defillade fire on the enemy guns from an angle the gooks hadn't expected. They had been in the tunnels sixty seconds and had almost missed the fight, but now the reassured platoon poured fire and grenades onto the enemy and the RTO called in a gunship strike. They rolled all their CS gas grenades down the holes and the fight was over in much less than the hour it took the CO and the rest of the company to slog into the hills and relieve them. The cost was six dead and twelve wounded out of Dirty Dave's twenty-man platoon; only Dave, B-2, and the RTO were unscathed, though the RTO had the shakes.

The CO forgot the toll when Dave had them haul into the sunshine the footlocker full of money. The split was fairly made with only Dave's plat and the CO getting double shares. But American soldiers are greedy and even that fair split wasn't good enough for some who yakked their heads off back in base camp. What had been reported to the Batco as a sensational fight and victory without mention of the money suddenly became a treasure hunt for the Batco and

the military police, the Mamas and Papas. The company
was quarantined, shaken down, and two million dollars in
green and gook recovered, not counting what the MPs and
the Batco stuffed in their pockets before the count began.
Only a few of the company had had the foresight to hide
their spoils of war immediately after returning to base, and
those now didn't dare tell the others of their good fortune.
Three of them finally made it home alive with their shares,
joining the army cooks (who had sold army meat on the
black market and then served their men the cheap, infected
local beef and pocketed the difference) and senior NCOs
(who went partners in cathouses that served both Yanks
and Chucks) as men who had made profits on the war. B-2,
for some reason sensible only to his greed, believed the
army had stolen from him $150,000 in spoils, his calculation
of what he had in his pockets when the Batco brought in the
MPs. That was his legal share plus all he had stuffed into his
pockets before the CO had divvied up. He meant to have it
all back. The army could recompense him by giving him
another shot at some spoils or he would do the American
thing and sue the army for his money. Either way was fine
with him so long as he got his share. That was his Purpose
in the war.

The trail grew rougher and stormier as Bravo Company
climbed the mountainside; the rougher trail gave them
better footing. The rain slackened and blew away with the
fog and suddenly the mountain, old and humpbacked,
called Old Baldy, stood out in sharp relief against the velvet
black sky and its stars. The sudden end of the rain frightened the Mikes up ahead. They opened fire against the
mountain with everything they had.

Cursing, B-2 flung himself down alongside the captain
and Waldo. The FO had his radio on and was ready to call
fire, but the tracers skittering back over the company were
good American orange tracers and not enemy green.

"Georgie Bee!" shouted the captain. "Tell 'em to stay down and don't shoot unless I say!"

"It's just the damn Mikes, Captain," the Bee replied. "We won't hurt 'em."

Waldo turned off his radio and lay back on his pack. He was shaggy, unshaven, and hungry again. His arms and legs were torn and battered by tree limbs, thorns, and razor-sharp elephant grass. His mind was tired, his spirit bruised. Forty-two lives depended on him: He was the man with the big guns. He believed there was nothing his artillery could not do; he was the Bravo's bodyguard with 133 days to go on his tour. But he felt like a man who has used up all his strength and luck in mistakes and still must face the dragon.

Captain Daddy, the Missouri parson, squeezed Waldo's arm, saying, "It's okay, boy, it's okay. Ya just gotta cope," and surprised Waldo back into the war.

The ridiculous racketing riflefire upslope degenerated into yips of pain as the Mikes came tumbling back downtrail wide-eyed and hysterical. "Let 'em pass, let 'em pass!" shouted the captain. "And good riddance to 'em." The GIs shouted insults, tripping the Mikes with their rifles. Down by the rear guard where Sar'n Mars held power the GIs slammed the arrogant martinet Mike captain against a tree and beat him for a coward. The captain was pleased with his blood and bruises; they would support his lies about his single-handed battle with Chuck.

With the Mikes gone and nothing ahead but the star-glittering night and the mountain, Captain Foley led out, whispering for Fruitcake to fall back to report. After all that noise, they'd have to cut new trail now to avoid Chuck zeroing in on them with mortars. Fruitcake made no response. They found him shot through the head by a Mike M16. The round had done the explosive damage that only a sinister little 16 can do.

Waldo, Daddy, B-2, and Georgie Bee stood over the

wreckage of what had been their comrade, the country boy. It was a cold and tearless send-off; soldiers waste no tears in the field. "What'll we do with him?" asked Waldo. (Great God, he thought, I've failed again! One after the other, I lose them.)

"We'll have to leave him here," said the captain. "We can't call dustoff and we can't detail anyone to carry him back down." He ran two gloved fingers over his eyes magnified behind his thick lenses held onto his face by the little strap.

B-2 bent over the corpse. "You'll have to take his things, Daddy, just so's those stinking Mikes don't come back and rob the bod. We don't want Chuck to get his weapon, ammo, or boots, either." (It's all accident, mistake, and luck, isn't it? he marveled. There's no skill in war. You're cannon fodder or you're not, dead or not. You find a million bucks or you don't.)

Georgie Bee took Fruitcake's M16 and handed it to Waldo. "A souvenir from Vietnam," he said. He began to cry. He squatted by the blown-up head and touched Fruitcake. That was all the ceremony Fruitcake had; there would be time and peace enough for more back home, after the body had been recovered, washed, salted and iced, and stuffed in its black plastic bag, cased twice, and airmailed to Mama. Foley took off his bush hat: "You were a good boy," he said, and put it on backwards. He forgot that he was wearing his glasses and tried to rub his eyes again with the black-gloved hands and punched his fingers into the glass. B-2 pulled off one of Fruitcake's dog tags and handed it to the captain: "I'd better cut trail now, Daddy," he said, trudging into the elephant grass. Peepsite came forward to take over B-2's bodyguarding of the captain. He turned his stricken, lopsided face from the corpse and said, "I never want to be here again."

Georgie Bee knew he had no reason to squat beside the body bawling silently—he considered himself a suicide on his second life—but it all came out of him. Waldo clapped him on the shoulder and said, "Shake it off, Bee, we're in Chuckie's country. Ya gotta be alert." The Bee left Foley and Waldo to arrange the body in a respectable way and to urge on the company. Each man came past Fruitcake's ruin in somber thankfulness that it was Fruitcake and not him, and each determined to shoot a stupid Mike first chance he got.

Waldo pulled himself to his feet from the trail mud and watched the leading elements of Bravo plunge upslope toward the downed chopper. "I am the one," he cried out silently to the night. "I'm responsible for them and I fail them. Will they all die because of me?" Trembling with cold and fear of failure, he settled the pack frame on his back and strode uptrail with his charges. He was the redleg, the artilleryman; his redemption depended upon bringing them back alive.

This was the price of his redemption from murder. The people of a nation tell their soldiers that war is not murder but justifiable homicide. The Fifth Commandment is suspended. Nevertheless, the first killing is always murder. None of the killing that comes after means as much, nor is it as difficult. Waldo's sin was failure of himself; his crime was murder; the longer his war lasted, the greater the chance to cleanse his darkened soul.

It was the seventeenth day in his war. His first combat mission. His new army mustache tickled (later he grew bored with it and shaved it off). He was filled with fear of showing his own incompetence but the cool professionalism of the Hawkeye pilot relieved him. The pilot had eight months in the war on this tour and had had three spotter planes shot out from under him; he was an old-timer who knew what he was doing, steeled in the horrors of the Bong Son Plain, where years earlier PFC Willard Mars had learned his war lessons. Waldo wanted desperately to make a good show for this old-timer to prove himself a man. "That's the Song Ba we passed over?" Waldo asked into the intercom, peering down from the backseat of the little plane at the river as slick and black as obsidian pouring between scruffy brown hills.

"Rog. What's our laager now?" said the pilot.

"We're, uh, off the map!" Waldo frantically unfolded the map in hopes of finding some part of it that showed him where they were. "We're off the map and out of my arty range," he said tensely. He pushed his nose flat on the plexiglass window, peering down at the riverbank where hundreds of fishing poles were jammed in the soft earth. Enemy fishing poles!

"Yep," said the pilot, twisting the Birddog around and up to seven-hundred-feet. Waldo's stomach twisted around and up with it. He began to sweat in the cold of the little cabin, wind whistling through the thin, worn fabric fuselage. He stared stupidly at the back of the pilot's drab flight helmet.

"This is still easy rifle range," said Waldo.

"Don't sweat it. I've lost three 'dogs and I'm still up here." The pilot lit a cigarette.

Waldo sank back into his seat, his flak vest chaffing his chin and wet armpits, his stomach full of vomit, his nose gasping for air, the heavy flight helmet causing his head to ache. The sweat matting his shirt to his chest and back turned cold.

"'Hey!" cried the pilot into the intercom. The plane spun over and dived at the black river. Waldo groaned as the bile rose in his throat. "There's a guy swimming in the river!" yelped the pilot. Waldo flattened his nose against the window and gaped down at the water. The windows shrieked; the engine clashed as the pilot swung the plane in wild pursuit down toward the water, the little aircraft swooshing down in a huge tubercular clatter, its fabric skin rippling, Waldo sweating, grating his molars, holding his turning stomach. "See him by the log?" shouted the pilot.

"Where?"

"Get a smoke!"

Waldo threw himself at the grenade rack, his fingers pulling every wrong strap, sweat stinging his eyes. He yanked wildly and the smoke grenade fell into his lap. He yanked the ring, shoved the grenade through the narrow side window, and held it at arm's length.

"Hurry!" shouted the pilot. "Drop it, drop!"

Waldo flung the grenade at the river. It burst early and a purple cloud gushed up toward the plane. The plane bent and leaped around like a cat after a mouse, orbiting back on the man swimming in the river.

"I don't see the smoke anymore!" cried Waldo.

"You threw it in the water, you idiot! I see him—he's swimming for shore!" The pilot threw the plane forward and Waldo slapped against the belts holding him in his canvas seat. "Forget the redleg, Waldo. This guy's mine. I'm gonna let him have it with the rockets!"

"But he's just swimming!" Waldo blurted out. "You can't kill a man for that!"

The startled pilot yanked the plane away from the attack, the cigarette once dangling from his mouth now jutting up, smoke from his nostrils clouding the windscreen. He twisted around angrily in his seat. "What's the matter with you? He's not supposed to be down there, right? This is a free-fire zone, right? So he's not a friendly, right? So we kill him, right?" The pilot swung back to his controls, angry. "All right, Waldo, you're the redleg this flight, so this mission is all yours. I'm just the driver. You tell me what we do."

Seventeen days into the war and Waldo was still full of untested American decency. He had not yet killed a man. But here was the moment peering up at him from a black river.

"It's all up to you," said the pilot firmly.

"Up to me?" cried Waldo. He shivered. He thrust his arms across his chest for warmth. How could it be so cold at just seven-hundred-feet? Sweat streamed over his face. Waldo saw that he was caught in the trap he had made for himself. The thought burst into his brain with unhappy certainty: Where is the justice in killing a man whose sole offense is to be caught swimming and vulnerable on the very day I happen to be hunting men to kill? What he learned in that moment is that no man should be killed in cold blood. That to go to war for any reason but desperation and there to kill is to commit murder. His soul began to shrivel in the moment he said softly into the intercom, "You're right."

"We've got him!" yelled the pilot, the plane flopping over and lining up on the river, the engine clattering, the wings shrieking. Black water, brown earth, and heat-shimmering trees spun across the windscreen. Suddenly the clatter and wail of the dive subsided. The pilot leaned into the windscreen. It was as though the plane was without an engine swooping into the obsidian stream to smash itself apart: It was quiet, still, no sensation of movement, nothing. Waldo sat like a statue as the plane dived down a five-hundred-foot cliff of air, a roller coaster racing downhill at its victim, the plane oddly stable, almost heavy.

Waldo jumped around in his canvas seat to see the four white phosphorous rockets hung under the wing. A lather of white flame! One rocket whipped off from the wing. He faced the river, looking over the pilot's shoulder through the windscreen as the pilot yanked back on the stick, the plane screamed up and around, and Waldo now saw nothing but sky and cigarette smoke curling out of the pilot's nostrils. He twisted in his seat and peered down at the water and suddenly his ears were filled with the sound of the rocket—*SSSHEEW!*—and the water and phosphorous rose up in a cascading silent blast flecked with magenta, chartreuse, and glittering silver.

His stomach was spinning, his mind circling. He was sure it was because of the plane's roller-coaster orbiting, the water falling back, the pilot leaning against the windscreen staring again at the black river and their target as the plane roared downhill, again becoming ominously heavy and stable and soundless, swooping for the kill.

"You see him, kid?"

"I don't see a thing," said Waldo, staring mesmerized at the white phosphorous fire splashing back into the river, spraying down on leaves and burning holes with its unquenchable chemical flame.

"There he is—I see him!"

The plane rocked over. Vomit rose in Waldo's throat; he trembled and sweated. The second white-smoking rocket jumped from the wing and Waldo twisted around to watch but it was gone. He jerked back to watch it impact in the river and saw it go slow and direct into the body of the enemy swimmer. The plane skidded right and up hard, skimming over the leaping blast that exploded in a brilliant WHOOSH! of color against the dark water, as though they had smashed stained glass, every bright bit caught in sunlight, tumbling, reflecting each spectrum. Waldo yanked off his helmet, held it in his lap, and threw up into it. He wept. The pilot heard none of it over the engine's clatter, saying, "Well, kid, scratch one Chuck. You just got your first kill and your first two hours of aerial combat time toward your Air Medal. Don't worry—you'll do okay from now on." He lit a second cigarette and passed it back over his shoulder. Waldo took it to drive from his nostrils the smell of his own vomit. They curved past Hong Kong Mountain, which stood half in and half out of base camp, glided over the broad barrier wire and napalm mines, and settled onto the Golfcourse. Waldo jumped from the cold cockpit into a hot afternoon, leaving the soiled flight helmet on the canvas seat. The pilot glanced at it in disgust as Waldo hurried away across the dusty steel-planked airstrip. He had suddenly become aware of the *whip-whip* of three choppers testing engines, of heavy trucks grinding down oiled dirt roads, of jeeps buzzing through grassy fields, of tin shower doors slamming shut echoing across the whole camp, and behind it all lay the lazy pops of the six base-camp howitzers firing a training mission north into no man's land. The oiled street was dusty in his nose, his eyes hurt in the too bright sun, his boots grated his ankles.

In the mess hall, where he went for coffee to clear the bile from his throat, Waldo found another new FO in his battered camouflage fatigues, eight days' growth on his face, a combat haircut, an illegal .38 revolver on his hip (his father had sent him that as the army would give him nothing), telling tales of his first combat patrol. But he hadn't yet killed a man and was entranced with Waldo's better story. They both sat in the greasy mess hall, sweat dotting their jackets, the stench of rotted fish on the breath of the Viet KP girls filling the hall. Halfway through the telling of his adventure, Waldo had heard enough from his own mouth and got up and walked out, his story unfinished. He went into the showers behind his tiny slum barracks, turned on the icy water and stepped under it, rubbing his fingers over the veins throbbing at his temples, the muscles straining his neck. He peeled off his clothes and boots under the cold water; after an hour his spirit was numbed.

3

BRAVO SLOGGED ONTO the crest of Old Baldy, dragging their packs and rifles, exhausted. They had made two-thousand meters in five hours, a good day's march but an incredible accomplishment at night in Chuck's country. They stared down from their perch at the highway far below, the lights winking occasionally from the bunker doors of LZ Action there in the hideous maw of Mang Yang Pass and of LZ Schueller seven miles east. Farther east were the city limits of base-camp outside the highland village of An Khe, swollen with refugees. A transport plane swung down out of the sky and skimmed to a halt on the Golfcourse in front of the limegreen control tower built by the French legionnaires. The flyboys preferred night flying; they were afraid of Chuckie's .50 MGs that worked by day. A flashlight blazed an instant on Bridge 25, where twenty GIs and a couple of tracks hunkered down behind their wire barricades and sandbag bunkers to keep the Chucks from blowing the bridge in his night. It was Bridge 25 that had reported seeing the chopper go down in the saddle between Old Baldy and Hill 415.

They turned to face south off the mountain and peered into the lightless murk of the valley where Chuck lived. God, Lucifer, Judas, all those the army is; it is also the good shepherd who, one of its hundreds lost, will leave the flock to find the lost sheep. Mother Army peered off that mountain into Chuck's grim night face and though there was fear in them all, there was no doubt in them that they would fulfill their sacred mission.

Captain Foley took the hand phone from the hand of his uptight RTO, Kansas City, and called higher on blueleg net: "We're diggin' in here at our laager for the night. The boys're bushed and I can't risk 'em in a fight in the open without some rest, over. . . . Roger that. We move out at 0430, out." Foley turned to his one lieutenant and executive officer, First Lieutenant "Bad-Henry" H. Harvey, an ex-baseball player who might have made pro if the draft had not caught him, a big bluff man with an infectious smile that ran to a rapid twitch if held too long, and fingernails as constantly grease-filled and uncleanable as a garage mechanic's. "Dig in—slit trenches—we stay here tonight—no cook fires except in the holes, and make sure the boys hunker down with ground cloths over the holes if they do want to cook—we move out in four hours."

Waldo turned away from the wall of black that lay behind Old Baldy. "The gunbunnies won't like to lose the sleep, but I'll have 'em drop a flare in the valley every twenty minutes just so the chopper knows we're still comin' for 'em."

"Good idea," said the captain. "Give 'em some hope." He pulled off his glasses and rubbed the eyes swollen from the night march. "I told higher where they could find Fruitcake's body at first light. They'll have the minesweep tank collect it. Sar'n Mars, one man in three sleeps. You and Lieutenant Bad set out the MGs and claymore mines. Make it fast—we got four hours' sleep and we're lucky to get that—I want you both rested as well as the men. Waldo, tell me again—how many tubes can we call on the Valley?"

"LZ Action's got six 105mm howitzers, Captain. Schueller's got six more but they can't range more than five miles south of Baldy because they're farther off. They also got two eight-inch howitzers there and they can cover us as far as we can walk."

"Good enough," said Foley. "We also got some air cav next door and we can call on them for support."

With his order of battle set and his night orders given, Captain Foley turned from his two lieutenants—Waldo and Bad-Henry—and his sergeants, faced the valley, and began his prayers as the others drifted off to their duties. It was no Gethsemane of prayer; it was an honest man's prayer—he prayed for deliverance for himself and his boys and then he shut up and let the cosmos have its way. He slept deeply, the only one who slept well that night.

Waldo gouged out his sleeping hole and ate cold muck from cans. Tomorrow night, perhaps, they'd dig in a real forward operations base (FOB) and he could pop some heat tabs or a bit of plastique and boil up some Lurp rats and eat well, like rice and chicken boiled together and perhaps some dehydrated peaches. With a taste of stale GI powdered coffee and a bite from Mars's bourbon canteen, he would then sleep the sleep of a Roman emperor after his feast.

Waldo rolled under his poncho, easing the .45 automatic from his rucksack, cocking it, flipping on the safety, and laying the weapon on a green handkerchief (to keep it off the dewy earth) on the grass. He put his bush hat over it. He pulled his radio and Fruitcake's M16 against himself in the bedroll. He took out his six-inch campknife and stabbed it in the earth by the pistol. The army had given him his pistol but he had had to buy his knife and to steal most of the other gear he carried or wore. Batteries for his radio he bought from rear-echelon troops by trading them counterfeit NVA belt buckles with those fancy stars on them. Fruitcake's life had bought Waldo his rifle. He huddled in his bedding and ran his hand across the grass separating him from his slit trench to check the distance he'd have to roll if mortars started coming in. Then he ran his hand through the wild jet black hair that he could never keep combed. He lay back under a velvet darkness, his nose testing the scents of earth, water, trees; he listened to the wind; the air felt like autumn after a shower; the trees around him were bare from defoliant. Orion stood low on the horizon. On some distant hill a tiger yowled like a baby crying. Waldo wanted a woman. A woman with laughter and long hair to lie there with him to see and smell and taste everything he could. A woman who could remind him of the man he could now barely recall as being himself, a man who, in some far time and some distant country, had been a better man than the Waldo he now knew. He drifted into bottomless sleep and woke to the scratching of a brushbuck in the deeper trees. He slept again. He woke as another man stumbled into the brush to urinate. He slept.

He woke with a start at the first flash of morning, expecting to see the others awake and crouched against the fearful first light, but he woke from deathly sleep with adrenaline forging through his heart. He snapped on his pistol belt and radio, snatching up his helmet and pistol, Fruitcake's 16, boots laced, maps in pockets, compass swinging on a shoestring from his neck, up and ready for war.

"They're coming for Fruitcake," yelled the captain, his outstretched arm swung out over the valley of Highway 19, its asphalt squeezed between fields of gray white lettuce and green jungle, two platoons of tracks and tanks racing in from the east, choppers diving from the Mang Yang bluffs west and, centered, an exploding minesweeper tank and another tank like a bedeviled hound dodging and churning past rockets and enemy riflemen and behind them the last dead American tumbling out of the bed of a blasted pickup truck.

"Oh Christ!" "Drop ya packs!" "Platoons on line!" Waldo snapped on his artillery net radio and shouted into the mike, "Yonkers three-one, three-one, this two-four, two-four, firemission, over!"

They plunged off the ridgeline and swept into the forest, hacking at branches with machetes and rifle butts, cursing the jungle, blasting off stray rounds in their frustration and shouting encouragement to the tank—a terrific blast behind the leaf wall—they dived through the brambles shredding clothes, dumping radios, throwing down canteens, and burst into the clearing, screaming, burning, and breaking with their bullets—but the tank was slumped and exploding again and again, arcs rising from it in flashes of yellow and green, the gun tube ruptured and cartwheeling into the trees, the turret split open—and the enemy was gone! Friends dead! Men fell sobbing in rage. Waldo, with the artillery radio and his rifle slung on his back, phone in one hand and pistol in the other, raised his .45 and fired it into the trees behind which ran the enemy. He fired and fired and fired until the magazine ran empty and the slide refused to close.

Sar'n Mars stood over the body of a dying Arvin grunt whose stumps of legs gouted blood. He had been thrown out of the back of the blasted pickup truck. "He's wasted," Mars reported in a shout. He opened the Arvin's shirt, found his dog tags and tossed them to the only intact member of the Arvin minesweep team who was staring transfixed at the pouring legs.

Already they were sanitizing the field of battle; the medevac choppers had swooped away the Yank and Arvin bods, the wrecker from LZ Action had towed the gutted tank out of sight down the road, the GIs had neatly stacked the enemy corpses on the road for the villagers to plunder, then shot the bods to pieces with autofire.

"Sar'n Mars!"

"I hear ya, Peepsite."

Peepsite, whose twisted nose and uneven eyes gave the

impression he was made half and half of two different men, slammed another mag into his 16. "I didn't have anything to do with this, Sar'n Mars!" He loosened another burst into the corpses and walked away toward the trees.

"I know ya didn't, Peeps."

"In fact, I'm not even here."

"That's right. You ain't here often."

The virgin forest was again serene, waiting.

"Let's go!" shouted the captain, motioning forward with his black-gloved fist, and the Bravos seeped away into the trees. In the chopper taking him to hospital, lifting them both out of war, the dying Arvin watched the last living member of his squad rob his pockets.

The Bravos turned their backs on the wreckage that was no longer their responsibility but the woman's work of the helis, and they went up the mountain and over into the Valley.

It was as though they had never slept, had never eaten. They trudged over Baldy with the bone-weariness of men doing the world's toughest work on the least sleep and food. A soldier is always exhausted, a forest animal forever in the season of starvation. He is poor and ragged. They went into the valley, forty-one weary infantrymen and one redleg, Waldo. The fighting soldiers are despised for fools by the rest of the army, those who are too smart to hump, clever enough to pull berths as clerk typists and mechanics. No one in the army loves a combat soldier but another combat soldier. That love is without expression, but it is sealed with this code: A man will lay down his life for his buddy and his buddy will do the same for him.

It was a bright summery morning, the grass green and yellow and only waist-high now. The bushes, leaves, and trees smelled fresh after the night's rain. They cut trail down into the valley across a dozen streambeds and found an enemy trail—while the meadow grass was six inches tall, that on the trail was worn to bristle and bare red earth. Captain Foley reported that to higher as the first gunships rocketed overhead, spinning out over the valley in the first good light of day searching for their downed comrade. These were a mix of Light Observation Helis (Loaches) and Cobras, the small two-man Loaches acting as eyes for the fierce but blind (because they fly so fast) jet-powered Cobra gunships. They were the air cav from the adjoining Area of Ops—which meant they were under no obligation to Foley. They were infamous for their bad coordination with the ground troops, and they were arrogant about it. The Bravos instinctively ducked their heads as these powerful machines swept over.

Cigarettes passed up and down the column; the men were surprisingly quiet. The flank guards left and right betrayed themselves only by the soft sounds of leaves rushing over cloth, and the occasional hack of a machete. The company entered a tangle of briars and came upon a stream with bamboo thick and tall all about. Here they were out of sight of the choppers and felt safer, though Chuck liked to ambush in such places. Foley split the company for security, the first platoon crossing upstream and the second meeting it at the clearing under the canopy of bamboo leaves. All they found were the bones of a water buffalo. The stream was cloudy gray but they filled their canteens, adding iodine, and drank. A brushbuck barked somewhere deeper in the throat of the valley; they pulled south, Sar'n Mars on point. Ants crawled up their trousers from the ground littered with leaves. Crickets chattered. The *caw-caw-caw* of a jungle bird. The helis and a Hawkeye pulsed past overhead.

Kansas City, the RTO behind the captain, was nervous: He was getting short, due to leave the country in six weeks. He was resentful and whined about still being in the field. He blamed Foley for his presence and had begun to nurse a fine hatred for his commander. He swung his rifle from side to side, watching, pushing through the brush wide-eyed with terrified alertness. He knew a soldier has only a finite amount of luck that drains away quickly; as he approaches his time to leave war, he has very little luck left to protect him.

Reginald Peepsite Taylor with his uneven face looked across at Waldo marching beside him. Waldo walked along in his field slouch straining under fifty pounds of rats and ammo and a Prick-ten radio, Fruitcake's rifle resting easily in the crook of his arm and supported by a utility strap over one shoulder, safety on but magazine loaded and chambered. The steel helmet that higher insisted they carry in the field (though no one used them) bonged against his shoulders with each stride as it swung on its strap from his pack frame.

Waldo dropped his hand to a thigh pocket, yanking out the plastic map and grease map pencil. He checked the map against the trail against the compass swinging from his neck on a shoestring. All corresponded. He sighed and put everything away. He marched another five minutes and did it all again. And did it all day, every day. The grunts had stared at him at first as, eyes flashing, head ducking, he clumped behind a shield of leaves offtrail. Waldo wanted no Chucks to see his map and shoot him for an officer; for the same reason he wore no insignia of rank and usually carried his officer's pistol in his rucksack instead of on his hip. He swept the map from his pocket, adjusted it to the terrain, snapped open the compass, measured his three directions, nodded to himself, and put it all away, doing it all like a nutty toy machine. The grunts got bored with his show and left him to it. On every side were trees and he climbed these often to look for Baldy and other points of interest to orient his map. Captain Foley was a lousy woodsman and would surely get them all lost, choppers overhead to help him or not. Getting them there and bringing them back was

Waldo's responsibility. That was how Waldo saw it, anyway. From all three directions.

The blue net radio crackled; Daddy took the hand phone
from Kansas City. "Oh Jeez!" he said, "Pass the word
back, Kansas—the choppers have found the wreck. Give
me your map, Waldo." Daddy mused over it, absently
holding the still squawking handset until Kansas took it
from him and, in trembling voice, finished the captain's
conversation.

"Air cav says it's down in thick brush at grid 532478.
That's here, right?" Foley stabbed a finger at the map.

"Over here, Daddy," said Waldo, snapping on his own
arty net radio to report the find to Fire Direction Control
(FDC) at LZ Action and to have them plot in defensive fires
around it in case they were needed when the Bravos got
down there.

"That's two klicks farther south," said Sar'n Mars,
glowering at the map, using his limp bush hat to wipe sweat
from his bald heat. "A day's march in *this* bush, minimum."

Foley blinked his huge magnified eyes at Mars. "Oh no—
the helis are gonna take us down. Three search teams of
three each. Lieutenant Harvey, I see something like a
clearing ahead of us on the map here. You take the point
with B-2, two MGs, half a plat and push on ahead and
secure it for us. We'll call down the choppers and meet you
there. Don't wanta give Chuck too much notice of our
presence. We've gotta be quick."

"Yo, Captain." Lieutenant Bad-Henry Harvey with his
ready, twitching smile and his baseballer's shoulders and
his eager troops, shaken from their sunbaked boredom and
streaming sweat, plunged ahead on a fresh adventure.

"These are the search teams," announced the captain to
the thirty faces clustering around him. "Higher wants
redleg out there just in case, so Waldo goes. That leaves

just eight slots." The GIs groaned. "One slot goes to B-2 for Waldo, another Sar'n Mars. Sar'n, you take Peepsite and Loopy. Georgie Bee to lead the third team with two riflemen. When we get into the clearing, ditch your packs with your buddies. Sling three bandoliers of ammo apiece. Waldo, I know you don't like hand grenades on your team, so you other teams take three hands apiece. One grenadier—you, Ayrab—go with Waldo. Sar'n Mars and Bee, I only got enough radios to give one to one of you—the other one stuff flares in his pocket and see if maybe there's not a loose Prick-ten in the chopper to steal. Got it? Good. Let's move."

They ran into the clearing under the fierce beat of the first chopper's blades—a Huey slick with a machine-gunner on each flank—and each team piled on board as, one after another, the three slicks dipped into the meadow that was barely fifty meters across and swooped up the teams. With them gone and his already half-strength company depleted by another quarter, Captain Foley started his remaining thirty-three men to work on foxholes, chopping logs for overhead cover, and setting up tiny mortar pits for the two 60mm mortars they'd brought with them. The sixty isn't authorized issue for a straight-leg company but Foley had bought them for his boys, and the ammo, from a top sergeant he'd caught pilfering beer from the base camp PX to resell to GIs and Chucks in the cathouse he owned. For his freedom, the NCO paid happily with two 60s he stole from a Green Beanie A-Team, who refused to take the field when there were common soldiers to do their work instead. Then, less happily, he continued to supply Bravo Company with the ammo for the privilege of continuing to pilfer from the PX.

Foley let them make cook fires to eat—after the choppers had given away their laager to the Chucks, it made no sense to maintain the strictest security. And there was the air cav

overhead to help them if things hotted up. The birds
chirped, the crickets sang, deer bolted across their perimeter, and they whiled away the hot day listening to transistor
radio music from Hanoi, a ring of soldiers and weapons just
inside the trees (good protection from enemy mortars)
guarding the precious little meadow on which the choppers
would land to bring their buddies back to them or to extract
the Bravos if necessary.

Waldo had dived under the rotors of the first slick, its
skids jumping on the grassy red earth like a thoroughbred
impatient to run, and he had barely scrambled on board
with B-2 and Ayrab, the dark and delicate Syrian immi-
grant, when the machine lurched into the sky, the diver
shouting over his shoulder, "We got the redleg back
there?"

"That's me" said Waldo.

"You got it plotted?"

"Delta tangos at the cardinals. They don't want steel
now, do they?"

The driver shook his head and peered across the thin blue
sky as the slick swooped deeper into the valley. Their guide
was the first dead man. The side gunner had leaped from
the falling chopper and was skewered on the tip of a young
pine tree. Waldo and the others looked out at it in sick
revulsion, watching Georgie Bee's team being inserted
there to pull him down, thankful it wasn't them.

They were there! "LZ's cold," shouted the driver sitting
on his armored seat, "so don't worry. Can't touch down—
earth's too soft after last night's rain—but it's good enough
for boots—get out!"

The chopper dropped to ten-foot altitude while the machine, afraid of enemy bullets and with the stink of a
chopper death in its nose, skittered there in the air. "Hey,
put us down farther!" shouted B-2.

The pilot shook his head. "No way—this place could hot up with all the attention it's getting and I don't want to be Chuckie's meat. Jump!"

Waldo was the first out. As he jumped he saw the wreckage of the downed chopper—a Huey slick with a red cross painted on its tail boom. It looked like a crushed grasshopper with only its tail left whole. It was reduced to ash. He tumbled through long, rotor-beaten space to earth, landing on his feet and sinking to his knees in swamp covered with a thin crop of grass. "Hey! Hey!" he shouted up at the black polliwog skittering above him. "Don't jump, you guys! Bring that thing down here!" But it was too late—B-2 was leaping into space. His foot caught on the skid as the heli bounced, and he cartwheeled down on top of Waldo, and Ayrab with his M79 grenade launcher and three bandoliers of snub-nosed, bulletlike grenades fell on them. They thrashed around in panic in the sucking mud, helpless and in clear fire from the trees, as the chopper lifted away. They dragged and shoved each other, panting, to hard ground among the tree roots, and watched—as they wiped sweat from faces and mud from weapons—the third heli drop Sar'n Mar's team a klick away.

Waldo put his radio on the company net and reported in: "We're down and see the others down—we're by the wreck and going in, out."

"Let's go," said B-2, scrambling to a crouch, his always worried eyes grown large in their bruised sacks.

"I'm huggin' your tail, buddy," said Ayrab, clutching the massive grenade launcher to his chest as he headed out behind Saavedra.

They fanned out ten feet apart and moved in on the wreck on skirmish line, moving like nervous woods creatures in hunting season. It took them thirty minutes of noisy and frightening machete work to get through the brush to the chopper. Flight manuals that had been torn apart and thrown up into the treetops when the machine had exploded drifted down around them page by page as they worked. Finally they broke into the hillside clearing burnt out by the chopper and stood staring at the wreck. Only the long boom of the tail was whole, its tiny rotor creaking over once or twice in an errant breeze. The body of the machine, the great glass and aluminum hull that made it look in flight like a polliwog, was reduced to ash, burned beyond recognition.

"I'll stand fast here," said Waldo. "You two fan out left and right around the clearing and recon. Keep in the treeline, but keep in sight of me and each other." They moved out into the brush. If there were any Chucks around, then Waldo's team was already bushwhacked. Or at least Chuck would have booby-trapped the wreck. Ayrab whistled softly, and they all moved out of the trees to surround the machine.

"Spotted what might be a blood trail over there, leading north-northeast, up toward Sar'n Mar's team."

Waldo called Mars to report. The others stared at him to avoid looking at the wreck. "Okay," said Waldo to them, clicking off the handset of his radio, "let's search this thing and the woods around. Keep an ear cocked for Chuck." They still stared at him, unwilling to face the horror their mission had brought them to find. "Let's go." Waldo led out.

It was not much of a search. The fire had left little to sift through. There, in the frame of the cockpit window, on the left side where the copilot sat, staring out of the ash at them, was a skull in its helmet. There was nothing else. The fire had been quick and hot and had taken everything else, leaving only the protected skull in its armored helmet resting on the armored shield that every pilot sat on. "I never wanta fly in one of those things again," said B-2.

"How you gonna get outa Chuckie's valley today? Ya wanta hump it alone?" said Ayrab, turning away from the skull.

Waldo said, "Fire like that burned so fast he was dead before he knew it."

"I hope the crash knocked him out first," said B-2. "Damn. What a way to go. Some guys got no luck at all."

Ayrab loosed a shuddering sigh. Without turning to face the skull, he said, "We got none, either. Why couldn't we have found a live one? Who's gonna pick up that skull?"

"Dead is dead," said B-2. "His mama'll want this." He plucked the helmet from the ash and pried out the skull. Singed flesh and hair stuck inside the helmet, the reek a bitter meat stink. B-2 dropped the mess, turned, and ran for the woods, where he threw up, falling on his knees with the power of the convulsions. Ayrab turned his head to avoid seeing either the skull with its bloody, hairy crown or B-2 retching.

Waldo unrolled the poncho he had tied to his pistol belt. He gingerly picked up the skull and rolled it in the plastic sheet, looping the roll around one shoulder and tying the ends. Ayrab finally turned to face Waldo. "Let's eyeball the woods," said Waldo. There they found the second thing, stretched out like a figure from Pompeii caught at its moment of death, arms flung out, not even dog tags remaining. They would have kicked through it without recognizing it—it was nothing more than crucified ash—but two of the long bones remained, shrivelled and blackened, and ten feet farther into the trees was the pilot's helmet with his name on it. Waldo wrote the name in grease pencil on his plastic map, the map that was more sacred to him than his dog tags; he would be dead before he'd part with it. B-2 had come back, clutching his stomach, his 16 in his free hand. Ayrab unrolled his poncho pack and did as Waldo had done. He picked up the two femurs between thumb and forefinger and rolled them in his poncho. "What do we do about the ash, Lieutenant?" he asked, his face running bloodless. He fixed bright glittering eyes on Waldo and said, "We oughta do something about the ash."

"Bury it," said B-2.

"We'll take it," Waldo said. "Unroll your poncho, B-2."
B-2 stared at him, stricken, then unrolled his poncho and
laid it by the ash figure.

"I'll do it," said Ayrab. "I already got it on my hands."
He scooped up the ash in cupped hands and filled the
poncho, his breath coming higher and sharper as he
worked. He stood up with shaking hands as B-2 tied the
plastic sheet and looped it around his waist so nothing
would be lost. Ayrab shook off the ash and wiped the last
paleness on his fatigues and said, "Let's go!"

They went along the blood trail, Waldo calling ahead to
Sar'n Mars that they were coming and reporting what they
had found.

The formula for war is thirty days of boredom and thirty
seconds of terror from which the soldier slogs back into his
numbing boredom. Patrolling was a special bore to Staff
Sergeant Willard Mars, and without his mission to see the
young men of Bravo through the war, he would have been
content to take what was rightfully his and abandon the war
to the young men. After four years in war, Mars could have
any billet he wanted in base camp, where he could eat, find
sex, drink himself into contentment; that was his due. But
there was something special that kept bringing him into the
woods: He loved Vietnam. Not the Vietnam on the map—
that place existed on another planet, Uncle Chuckie's
planet, a place where the Department of Procurement
turned its profits and no place Mars ever wanted to see. No,
his Vietnam was the Vietnam of bright cool country where
no man had ever been before, where the tigers had no taste
for human blood and where the ground was not polluted
with jump-up bombs, where each color was a shade lighter
than he'd expected, where the sun was everywhere in thick
sheets, cutting, curving, cornering between the forest trees
filling all that brisk terrain with flapping, screeching life,

pushing out of his mind demon memories of dead men and the family he'd abandoned in Burgerland. This land he now walked had belonged to Frenchmen who lay rotting beneath his tread. He thought of that, too. Yet now, plodding along a trailless jungle hoping for survivors of the downed chopper, he could not think of them or of death. In the quiet lushness of the forest beneath the old round-shouldered mountains on the crystal horizon, Vietnam seemed an unlikely place to die. He was clean, healthy, vibrant, virile, terrified, breathing gritless air, shielding his eyes from jungle colors that were clanging bright, the cold ball of ever-present fear above his groin.

Peepsite Taylor and Jacob "Loopy" Doumitt (who had a child's fascination for everything), the riflemen, clucked and brought Mars out of his reverie.

"We got movement," Peepsite said in a low voice. He pointed south.

"Probably Waldo's team. They must have found him," Mars said. They moved cautiously through the trees.

"Let's hope it *is* Waldo, and not Chuck," said Loopy.

"I hear ya," Peepsite muttered.

They moved on in silence and came upon Waldo, B-2, and Ayrab staring at the ground.

"Blood trail ends here," said Waldo. "You find anything?"

"Nope," said Mars. "We better check out the ground. He's got to be here somewhere."

But they found nothing. No body. No trail. Nothing. Waldo called Captain Foley. "Daddy, we got a real dead end here. No bod, the blood trail just ends, over."

"Look like Chuck, over?" asked Foley.

"If it was, he'd have ambushed the chopper. Not even a booby trap there. I don't figure it at all. We checked it out, over."

"Tigers," Peepsite muttered nervously, gazing around at the forest.

"Listen," Foley said, "I've got to pull you out of there. The air cav is gettin' antsy, and you've been in there long enough to attract Chuck. I'll call for your extraction before the air cav finds something better to do with its helis, out."

"But what if he's out there alive somewhere, over?"

"Then he's MIA. I'm sorry for him, but that's better'n you six KIA. I'm bringing you in, out."

The air cav sent one slick for all three teams, and two Cobras for protection. The men from Bravo piled in with relief. Ayrab sat against the pilot's bulkhead, his fine, long-fingered hands ash white, staring white-faced and big-eyed at nothing. The skewered body Georgie Bee had brought down from the tree lay stiff, sprawled across the flooring; they piled the poncho rolls of bones on the white-eyed corpse to make room for themselves.

The heli jumped away from the LZ into the protection of its two Cobras. The pilot, seeing the spoils of the downed chopper, kept higher than necessary by hundreds of feet. The Bravos were ecstatic to be out of Chuck's country, if only for minutes, and to be safe up there beyond rifle range. They were also depressed, disappointed, wrung out, self-hating: They had gone looking for buddies to bring home and they had found a cruel joke instead. They had failed their buddies, and now one of them was MIA. It was as though they each believed that the power of his goodwill alone could save a man's life. They had failed because they were not the supermen they had to be.

"We're goin' in!" yelped Peepsite, his massive frame sitting on the floor of the chopper, his legs dangling out into space. Below them was Captain Foley with his nervous RTO, Kansas City, in the center of the little meadow, motioning to the heli. Peepsite was the first to be hit: His warped face twisted apart as he took a .30 MG round through the head, splattering himself all over the others. He bucked against the bulkhead and then was flung foreward into space, arms thrown out, screaming, falling on Foley as the others leaped out of the chopper that was already jumping away from the LZ without touching down—the driver wanted to be gone, and the grunts wanted out of that firetrap. They left the remains of the three dead men from the downed chopper in the custody of their own kind, hit the spongy meadow earth tumbling to their feet, grabbing up weapons, radios, Captain Foley and Peepsite, and ran for the treeline as the second burst of enemy machine-gun fire sizzled overhead, thunking through the light aluminum body of the chopper that was shrieking up out of range.

4

IT TOOK THE second enemy burst to shake the Bravo perimeter out of its separate reveries of the war's end and to open into the trees a clattering fire sharpened by the earsplitting explosions of half a dozen M79-launched grenades.

"Incoming!"

"It's a goddamn 82!" shouted Knobs, his bowlegs propelling him into a bunker.

"Inta yer holes!" yelled Mars. They could hear the bangs of the enemy tubes firing—three mortar tubes, close together and close to them—and that meant very high trajectories and that meant they had fifteen to thirty seconds to dive for cover while those big 82mm mortar rounds went up out of their tree hideouts, arced up a thousand feet or more in the clear sky, and then fell at them in a rushing, screaming blur that none of them wanted to hear.

"Damn good gunners!" shouted Waldo. They had Peepsite in their arms in Foley's half-completed bunker—the stink of damp earth and of freshly cut logs topped with the regulation three sandbags carried per man—three of them depended on that hole, so they had a semisafe layer of nine earth-filled, plastic-woven bags. Peepsite was blown to pieces; one round had gone side-to-side through his face and another had opened his chest. "I'm not copin' very

57

well," he whispered to the captain. "Who says dyin' don't hurt?" Waldo was up and out of the hole running broken-field around the bunkers—he wanted another place to hide, away from death.

"Get in a hole, Lieutenant! The mortars'll be here in two secs!"

A new round of mortar firing began.

"Where'd those bastards learn to shoot like that?"

"Where'd they get so much ammo?"

The men with the three tiny 60mm mortars Foley had wangled for the company were oblivious to the steel that was seconds away from them—they were doing their work: stripped to the waist, sweat-gleaming sunburnt backs, scrambling and yelling around the three circular mortar pits dug down just three feet—that was all the depth they had had time to accomplish—with each little mortar on an earth pedestal in the center. They adjusted and fired by the sound of the enemy tubes, their own little tubes sounding puny against the deep-throated discipline of the even firing of the enemy.

"Time's up!" Mars yelled.

The mortarmen dived into their circular pits and the first three enemy rounds blasted into the trees far beyond camp—the soldiers howling with laughter—the rounds shattering treetops and spinning woodchips and metal fragments like confetti into the open meadow. Foley had done well to put the Bravos in the trees to save them from mortars and rockets, though he had sacrificed the use of their MGs to do it.

"Chuck hasn't got our range yet!" shouted the mortarmen, leaping up to fire. The second barrage crashed down.

"Closer, Chuckie, but not good enough!"

"Ya-haaa!"

The mortarmen worked, ignoring the zinging bits of tree and metal.

Waldo dived into a half-made bunker full of white-eyed

grunts, his radio hand phone clapped to his ear and mouth with two shaking hands as he said calmly—very calmly because he knew it would do no good to excite Fire Direction Control in base camp, it would only slow them down—"Yonkers three-one, two-four, firemission, over. . . . From Delta Tango-alpha, battery in adjustment, three VC mortars, over." The trembling fear left his hands. The sweat of fright dried on his face. He was doing his work, he was a pro, and it would save him from fear. He stared at the grunts in the hole with him: One gaped at him wide-eyed; the other ground his face into the earth wall, praying aloud.

The fight was forty-five seconds old, the third barrage of enemy mortar fire slammed across the base, this time neatly placed in the meadow but still doing no damage, and no Cobras had come in yet, though Waldo knew Foley in the hole with the dead Peepsite had called for gunnies. Sixteen klicks northeast there was a battery of six 105mm howitzers, and its gunbunnies were leaping to their breaches with projos, called out of lethargy into the war again, adrenaline pumping, dreaming jungle dreams of their steel cracking open the filthy Chuck armies and saving Yankee lives.

Waldo crouched in the bunker with the two terrified grunts watching the sweep hand on his watch, the band looped through the pocket of his fatigue blouse with the face turned toward his chest to avoid sun sparkle, counting off the secs. At the mark of sixty seconds the radio crackled in his ear and the battery's FDC said, "Shot, over."

"Shot, out!" He raised his head from the hole and shouted across the racketing base: "Keep yer heads down! We've got U.S. incoming!" The grunts cheered.

Now it had begun! The great swinging battering of the enemy he despised—he despised Chuck not because he was the enemy or because Waldo had no sympathy for other soldiers thrown into this useless mess of war, but because if he did not kill Chuck, Chuck would kill him, and the Bravos who were Waldo's responsibility. If there is resurrection of the spirit, Waldo would have none of it if he failed his company. Already his soul was shriveled. He could afford to lose no more of it in failure.

It had happened on his sixty-eighth day in the war. The chopper on its pad had whined to life. Waldo had dived under the rotors as the grunt colonel, the Batco, gray hair streaming, yanked him inside and shouted, "You got arty now?"

Waldo nodded fast, clapping his hand to his free ear to block out the rotors and the gray-haired Colonel Peter I. Yoden, a man fat like a ballplayer gone to seed. Waldo spoke slowly and loudly into the radio. "Fire all Delta-Tangos for strongpoint seven north of highway, over!"

"Roger," said the radio voice, "Delta-Tangos north SP seven, out."

Waldo peered between his feet at the base camp falling away beneath the heli. At two hundred feet the air became frigid. The chopper lurched up to get out of small-arms range.

"Shot, over," said the radio.

"Shot, out," replied Waldo. "First redleg, Colonel!" he shouted. The chopper twisted around the low mountains and the strongpoint came in sight—two tracks and a tank exploding on the road, soldiers diving cowering into the weeds, VC streaming back into the trees, enemy rockets streaking over the hills, six more tracks racing down the highway to the fight.

The artillery slammed up huge clumps of earth and smoke in the predetermined defensive targets, and it struck again and again, tearing the earth, churning over the running VC. Waldo jumped to his feet, and the colonel shouted, "Sit down and strap in, you fool!" but Waldo's eyes peered through thick shell bursts, seeking out the scuttling enemy, and he shouted into his handset, "From target bravo, azimuth five–eight hundred, add two hundred!" It was lousy procedure, but it would work.

"Roger. Shot, over," said the radio. The steel burst along the full line of enemy retreat.

"Right on target!" shouted the colonel.

"Add a hundred, repeat!" Waldo yelled into the radio. He saw an image of the guns in base camp belching clouds of cordite. He felt the long narrow rounds rocket through the gun tubes on tails of gas. He stood behind the guns and saw the shells arc far out over the mountains and descend. Now his eyes in the chopper caught the rounds as the chopper dropped in a ragged, rapid, terrifying sweep onto the ground: He saw them burst up beyond the mountains like corks bouncing up from deep water, curving up beyond the jungle, striking toward the field, falling as Waldo fell in the helicopter, the shells piercing the earth in great cauliflower clumps of brown smoke, earth, and shattering steel. The chopper touched down and Waldo jumped out and ran onto the strongpoint: The bunker had been blown apart, the tank and two tracks in flames, bullets chunked into the earth at his sides. He flung himself down behind an ammo crate as the third battery of rounds *KRUMP-KRUMP-KRUMPED* into the brush, slashing, lifting, shrieking. He peered over the ammo crate at the cauliflowers of dust and smoke blowing to smog. He was calm again, no longer the hysteric of those first few helpless seconds, into his professional routine, calling radio orders in a soft voice, his eyes searching the field for enemies he had not yet killed.

The first Cobras swooped down over the SP firing into the trees long streams of buzzsaw minigun bullets, and Waldo called cease-fire to the artillery to let the gunships do their work. He saw blood on his hands and on his handset. He jumped to his feet in surprise and saw a naked red foot jutting out from behind the ammo crate that had protected him and he saw a soldier flung out on the front edge of the ruined bunker, sandbags fallen over him, his shirt soaked with blood and mucous. Waldo stared at his own hands and understood everything but felt nothing.

He turned back to the road with his red hands upraised and saw a dozen GIs groveling in a ditch there behind a flaming track and he suddenly realized that his ears heard nothing until the soldiers shouted, "It's gonna blow! Get ya butt down!" A sergeant dived out of his ditch for Waldo and threw him down. "Can't you hear? That son of a bitch's gonna blow up!" he shouted at Waldo and rolled him behind the smoldering tank as the flaming track exploded in a giant *WHAM!* blasting its metal sides flat as a ruined card house, kicking the heavy steel deck thirty feet into the air, exploding steel and smoke mushrooming into the gentle blue sky, the deck crashing down onto the rubble and kicking the warped .50 machine gun barrel-first into the mud. "That's Bo Sartain out there," said Waldo, showing the sergeant his red hands. "He's dead."

"Know it," said the sergeant. "Was with him when it happened."

Waldo was calm, the fear that terrified every minute of his life and kept him alive and threatened to kill him once again under control. He saw everything with an old man's eyes, as though he had seen it many times before in a long life. He looked back at the little hill that was the strongpoint with its ruined bunker torn open and Bo Sartain's naked red foot sticking up from the sandbags, and he wiped the blood from his hands and he did not mourn, because he could not afford mourning. Everything was consumed in staying alive.

The GIs got to their feet out of the ditch and did not notice what Waldo saw: The thick weed by the treeline parted and closed, parted and closed, parted and closed, a silent dance. He thought his hearing had left him again but he could pick out the sounds of boots scuffing the hard ground, tanks churning into the woods under the whine of the helicopter fire, the crank and grind of the wrecker on the highway tugging off the ruined tank and tracks. He saw clods of earth gouged up near the soldiers' boots, a breeze whip their clothes, them shouting, "Hey! Hey!" and then the overwhelming rattle of the hidden machine gun's fire, like a hundred baseball bats rapping on a door, and he saw the soldiers throw themselves backwards twisting and screaming in midair, flinging down their rifles, groveling in the weeds that continued to part and close, part and close, part and close.

Bullets kicked past his calves, ricocheted off the hard ground around him, cut through the aluminum track body behind him, spit their gassy tails in his face; he was the only American standing upright in the fire, standing watching the VC machine-gunner firing bullets at Waldo, the radio-carrying officer marked with the pistol on his hip, the one by the ruined track, the one oblivious to bullets, the one watching the machine-gunner trying to kill him. He saw everything and understood everything. He was not afraid. His brain moved at such speed that he could accomplish miracles of leaping and running between the sizzling flights of bullets, but he chose to stand as he was. The frustration, misery, dreariness, confusion, failure of war had stolen his spirit from him. He could live or die, it made no difference to him now; he could be satisfied with either; he would be tormented by either. He understood it all: The war had him. He did not move. He waited without expectation. The bullets came at him.

Waldo believed he survived that moment because he was a zombie who could have his soul back if he was a good soldier. The Bravos were his trial by combat.

"Heads down!" Waldo shouted again as the first six rounds of fifty-pound shells crammed with high-explosive rocketed over the little meadow around which Bravo Company huddled, the shells echoing with the high-altitude whir of jet fighters, and blasting into the trees, sending wood and giant chunks of metal *whip-whip-whipping* through the forest, clanging into trees and stone, billowing cauliflowers of leaves and dust. The overwhelming power of the impacts stunned the enemy gunners and for seconds there was no sound but the last overhead shrieking of a piece of steel flung out on a high arc deeper into the valley.

Then it started again.

"Those are good gunners," said Waldo. "Got discipline."

"Do it again, Waldo!"

His head barely exposed over the lip of the bunker, a steel pot he had found on it, he said into his handset: "Add one hundred, over."

"Add one hundred, out. . . . Shot over."

"Shot, out. Incoming!" shouted Waldo.

"Right on!"

The enemy battery smashed into the trees over the perimeter, fragments knifing into the sandbags and spilling them, men screaming with fright and wounds and outrage, and then the tremendous rattling *whoosh!* overhead of the six arty rounds. A cheer rose from the Bravos. The artillery *KRUMPED!* as one impact in the forest. Waldo shouted over the base: "Anyone see the mortar flashes? Anyone got a fix on 'em?" No answer. He scrambled out of his bunker.

"Get the hell under cover, Lieutenant!" Knobs cried from his bunker.

He ran into the meadow and fell to his knees by three enemy impact craters. The slope of the small crater walls proved he was firing his arty in the right direction, but how far? He used his campknife to find the nosepiece buried a few inches under the crater and then laid his knife along the crater wall to trace the angle of fall. "Kee-rist, Chuck's farther out there than I thought!"

"Waldo, you fool, run for it!" Sar'n Mars shouted from Foley's bunker, his jungle hat on his head covering the blood that ran down his face from his sliced bald scalp.

"Ain't you got ears, Lieutenant?"

The heavy sizzling downroar of the three enemy 82s burst in his ears—no time to run and he couldn't be caught standing upright—he threw himself flat on the grass, groveling in the rich red earth. The three rounds cracked down around him, the concussion driving air from his lungs, and he gasped like a suffocating man as it threw him into the air and crashed him and his radio back to earth. The rounds had come in and flung up into the air all their metal and rock, harmless to Waldo clutching the grass. Hot metal sizzled in flesh-cutting arcs beyond the impact craters, over Waldo, into bunkers and hiding men.

Waldo ran to the MG bunker nearest the mortars and dived into a mass of squirming arms and legs. He yanked the plastic map from his thigh pocket, did his guesstimate and called in to the impatient guns with a coordinate and ordered, "Battery range and deflection spread, over."

"I like that!" cried Mars, crawling bald-headfirst into the crowded bunker. "Plow up this jungle, Waldo." He sighted down the barrel of the machine-gunner's weapon.

"Shot, over!" said the excited FDC, six men who both fought the war and fought it vicariously with maps and compasses in their electric-blue lighted bunker.

"Shot, out. Here it comes," said Waldo.

"Eyeballs and steaks," said the machine-gunner, Loopy Doumitt, at his gunport staring with his child's fascination into the trees. "That's what all we want to see out there, Lieutenant. I don't want Chuck runnin' up here after me."

"Where are the gunships?"

"They'll be along," Mars replied. "This fight's just be-gun—"

"And they don't like to show until it's just about over."

A barrage of machine-gun and automatic rifle fire with the cracking of hand grenades burst from the trees on the east side of the perimeter, blasting leaves and twigs before it, and satchel charges thrown against a bunker's gunports blew logs and sandbags into the tree limbs. Mars leaped from Waldo's bunker and raced around the perimeter gathering a grenadier, a machine-gunner, and two riflemen. He drove them white-eyed through the chopping enemy fire and had to do everything himself: set them up in a bunker that could defilade the enemy, concentrate M79 and MG fire in the center of the enemy attack, and then shout for the 60s to switch fire over there to drop rounds barely inside the treeline on the enemy. Though the mortars were ineffective, cracking open high up in the treetops where their impact fuses caused them to burst, at least their noise and the flung-down metal would keep the enemy off balance.

Cobras at last swooped overhead, and Mars, with a radio on his back, switched up to their freak and heard Captain Foley there call the Cobras down on the Chuck riflemen, leaving the three enemy mortars for Waldo's artillery to bury.

"Keep firing! Keep yer heads down!" roared Mars. "Gunnies comin' in!" There was no cheer with that announcement, just a grim relief and mistrust.

The Dragonships of the air cav with their Loach escorts, their eyes, darted across the blue sky, jet engines wailing, and lined up one above the other on the instructions of their Loaches and dived in.

"Now ya gonna get it, Chuckie! Ha ha hoo!" yelled a GI, standing up in his bunker and loosing a magazine into the trees.

"Dragon two-one! Dragon two-one! I see 'em! Must be fifty or sixty!"

"It's eighty or a hundred, my man! Breaking right!"

"Let's spoil 'em! Whowee!"

"Two-two, climb to one thousand, we'll come in on three-three-oh with left break."

"That's what I'm doing."

"Two-one, rolling in. Get your little butt outa my way, boy!"

"Loach three, orbiting west."

"And keep that little M16 in your lap this time, Davey Crockett. Don't get in my way."

"Two-one, two-one, this Loach three, I see smaller element a half-klick northeast!"

"What a hunt today!"

"Makes up for the downed chopper!"

"Where are the white hats?"

"West of the clearing. Everything east is our meat!"

"Shut up and shoot!"

Mars racing along the perimeter froze in half-crouch as he saw the diving Cobras and cried, "Oh my God!" The Dragonships, their black shark bodies etched against the blue sky, swung their snouts at the jungle. "Hit the deck!" he screamed, piling into a bunker at the moment he saw tiny orange flickers at the gunships' flanks and seconds later heard the heavy buzzsaw whine of their miniguns, and then the noisy forest went abruptly silent: The first ship had already pulled up steeply, the second diving in underneath, when the clatter of steel-jacketed bullets rang around his ears, bullets cutting out cones of jungle, hacking through trees, gouging out *American* bunkers, shattering *American* bodies. Wild screams burst from the camp.

The dying Knobs wailed, pierced through both shoulders. He staggered up out of his bunker. His bowlegs buckled and he fell dead. The two Cobras swung up and around in great roller-coaster loops, spitting thousands of rounds into the trees and bunkers, each hot shell slicing through the jungle canopy and slamming itself against bone and flesh.

Across the clearing Chuck screams echoed the Americans.

Behind him, Mars heard the whine of another rotor and

spun around to another gunport to see a tiny Loach scuttle overhead, the pilot leaning far out of his plexiglass bubble to spray the perimeter with M16 fire.

"Please no please no please no!" wailed a GI scrambling for the jumphole to run out of his bunker.

Mars grabbed the GI's blouse and hauled him back in, shouting, "Stay down shut up don't move!"

"Those are miniguns!"

"So stay in there, idiot!"

"Rockets! They're killin' us!"

Orange flame cracked open in the forest, splashing the enemy guns. Chuck's screams became piercing howls. "Fire out the ports, everyone!" ordered Mars. "Chuck's running!"

"Am I on fire?" asked a GI standing on the jumphole. His hair was blazing. Mars leaped out of the bunker, wrapped the man's head in his own fatigue jacket, and threw them both on the ground as rifle fire zinged over the meadow.

In the center of the meadow with his RTO groveling in terror at his feet and B-2 Saavedra on one knee bodyguarding stood Captain Foley, his steel pot thrown back on his head, his shirt drenched in Peepsite's blood, holding a purple smoke marker in one hand, his other fist thrust into the air at the Cobras, shouting, "You bastards! You bastards!" The last of Chuck's fire took him.

The Latin cowboy went berserk. He charged rage-blinded across the base, firing his 16 in endless bursts, changing mags on the run, spraying GI bunkers, spraying at the Cobras, plunging into the fire-gutted and meat-stinking forest with his rifle on go-go, screaming incoherent oaths, and he ran into the last steel rain from the Dragonships and was torn to pieces. The Dragons vanished into the sky.

The prevailing westerly breeze blew the gunsmoke from

the meadow, along with the bitter taste of cordite and the stink of burned flesh. "Cease firing!" shouted Bad-Henry, now in command. The massive lieutenant strode across the meadow oblivious to the last Chuck fire and rolled the captain's corpse off the cowering RTO. "Get up, Kansas, call us some dustoff, then get me batt."

"Yezzer."

"Mars! You alive?"

"Yo, Lieutenant! Over here."

"How's your radio?"

"Working."

"Check troops. Casualty and ammo list. Fast."

"Yo!"

"Waldo!"

The FO clambered up out of his bunker, the hand phone still clamped to his dirty face as he ended his firemission. "Here, Bad."

"Tell your higher I figure it was two companies come at us, the cowards wouldn't've used less. Tell 'em I want the D-Ts ready for firing asap on my command."

"Rog."

"Georgie Bee! Knobs!"

"Knobs is dead," said the Bee, getting to his feet inside the treeline. He wasn't about to make himself a mortar target there in the clearing with Bad. He was covered in mud, leaves stuck to blond crew cut, burst sunblisters draining over his red forehead.

"Okay, everyone—stand fast and keep your eyeballs and ears peeled forward. We're gonna get us some slicks in here and we're goin' home." Sar'n Mars strode into the clearing with Bad and Kansas, who had risen to his knees jabbering on the radio. "What's the bad news, Sar'n?"

"Twenty-one effectives, Lieutenant." Mars had a green bourbon-soaked handkerchief clamped to the bloody gouge on his bald head.

"Christ. We lost that many guys? We've been destroyed!"

"Seven KIA, four of 'em in the bunker that got blown plus Knobs and B-2 killed by choppers. Plus Daddy. Then twelve wounded—including all the mortarmen—"

"I'll put those bastards in for the BS, you know."

"—and most of them a credit to the Dragonships."

Lieutenant Harvey gazed around him in helpless fury, the tic coming onto his lips without the usual prompting of a smile. "What we got left for armament?"

"Lost one MG, that's all, and one radio."

"I'd rather have a radio than an MG." Harvey spat on the earth. "Let's tighten up the perim and hunker down. We oughta have them dustoffs in a minute and right behind them the slicks to get us outa here. Whadya say we have a look out there in the trees."

"We oughta do that but it's damn dangerous."

"Rather lose a patrol now than lose a chopper later and have those flyboys tell us we are on our own and we can hump out."

"Right. I'll go."

"Naw, I need you. You stay. Gimme three gunmen. Tell the troops I'll keep in radio contact with you and they're to ask your permission before firing, just in case it's me they want to blow away. I'll do my best to keep in visual range."

"They mighta dumped some booby traps out there. Be careful."

"I always am. Do somethin' decent with the corpses, Sar'n." Bad trudged off to sling on more bandoliers and a radio and went into the woods with his gunmen.

"Dig yaselves in!" Mars shouted to the company. "We might have ourselves a wait. Bee, ya got graves registration duty. Pile the bods someplace safe."

Waldo squatted just inside the treeline, plotting more defensive targets on his map and calling them in to FDC.

Mars squatted next to him, pouring more bourbon from his canteen onto his army-issued handkerchief and bathing the still-running wound on his scalp.

"FDC says dustoff on the way, Sar'n, and they put up another stick of Cobras to protect 'em," said Waldo.

"Not those same two from the air cav?"

"Naw, these're *our* Cobras, the Crocodiles."

"Peep's dead, ain't he?" asked Mars.

"Far as I know."

"So that's eight KIA. Well, he's finally not here. Good luck to him wherever he is."

"You been in this valley before, right?"

"Lotsa times," said Mars. "Feel like I was born here."

"What's the best way out?"

"North. The way we came in. What're you thinkin'?"

"I'm thinkin' we're in the wrong place at the wrong time," said Waldo. "I'm thinkin' that it's curious that your Batco sent this company at night to look for a downed chopper. He ought to have waited for dawn. Send out choppers and have them put a rescue team on the ground when they spot the wreck. That would be SOP. It's curious that your Batco's about to rotate home and he's not got his Legion of Honor yet. Maybe he wants us to buy it for him."

Mars stared back into the woods. "Well, I seen a lot of stinky stuff in this war and I seen that once or twice. Who's the enemy in this part of the Valley, Waldo?"

"The NVA Yellow Division and the 95-Bravo Chuck Regiment, plus some ragtag elements."

"Lotta guys."

"Could be five-thousand."

Mars groaned. "We know where they are—the regimental CPs anyway?"

"We got a few ID'd. But we don't like to come into this valley so most of 'em are anybody's guess."

"You could do that, couldn't you?" said Mars. "Sort of

infiltrate one company down here in the dark, then mark 'em by sending' choppers in to 'em, and let that company attract whoever's nearby. Decoy work."

"Then you send in four-to-five batts with some good arty support and gunships and stir up a real fight. Rotate home in a blaze of glory, couldn't you?"

Mars chuckled thinly. "Ya could, ya sure could. I think we've done our share for the colonel's glory, though. Even he knows it's time for us to go home. He'll get us out. We'll be sleepin' in base camp cots tonight."

Waldo and Mars stared with quick-moving anxious eyes into the trees. "Or it could be that Chuck will let those three dustoffs in and out because he wants to see us go home and leave him alone down here." Waldo said. "When he finds out we're still here, he's not gonna like it. *If* we're still here."

"Sar'n Mars!" shouted Kansas City, still cowering in the meadow. "Dustoff!" He pointed at the first of three medevac slicks dropping from high altitude searching for the meadow.

Mars ran into the clearing and broke open a purple smoke. "Get those wounded over here fast!" he shouted to Georgie Bee. The first chopper had barely touched skids to earth when the Bee's crew began lifting the moaning wounded onto the floor of the slick. The helicopter was off in fifteen seconds. They did it twice more and evacked a dozen WIA and the stack of eight dead. The air was suddenly peaceful without the cracking of the rotorblades, and the sky was empty.

"Where's the ships comin' for us?" the Bee asked.

"Batt," interrupted Kansas City, thrusting the handset at Mars.

Mars listened with tightening lips, said, "Roger, out," and gave the phone to the RTO. "We're stayin' put." Georgie Bee gasped. "They're sendin' in Action Company to join us if they can do it before dusk."

The Bee grabbed the mike from the RTO and held it out to Mars. "Tell 'em we gotta get outa here! Tell 'em they've pinpointed us for Chuck with dustoff! Tell 'em what'll happen to us tonight!"

Mars waved off the handset. "They know all that. That's why they're sending' in Action."

"But—us, a third of a company, and Action—against what the gooks got in this valley—a division and a half?"

"They know it." Mars glanced at Waldo still squatting there in the safety of the treeline with his map and radio, the blue eyes beneath that jet black hair stricken now: He had known what was coming but he had not wanted to believe it.

Lieutenant Harvey came out of the trees shouting for the perimeter not to shoot him. He and the others had mud and bloody gunk on their boots and trousers. They'd brought back a few souvenirs—a brass VC belt buckle, two Ak47 automatic rifles, and some satchel charges the company could use itself. He strode up to Mars: "I heard it, Sar'n, on the radio. What does batt think it's doing?"

"We're winning the colonel his Legion of Honor," said Mars, his voice vacant and worried.

"Hope he spreads around some of his glory." Harvey glared fiercely into the trees, squaring his baseballer's shoulders, biting his twitching lips.

Waldo came out of the protection of the treeline to join them. "When Chuck realizes we all didn't abandon this base in those three dustoffs, he's gonna come down here again and the slicks aren't going to extract us when he hits. One way or the other, we're gonna be stuck here by ourselves all night. I say we move out now while we can to a new laager and dig in. When night falls, we move out again and set up ambush-style, no holes, and be ready to fight and run north if we have to."

"You're thinkin' like an FO, Waldo," said Harvey. "You guys are trained to fight on your own and do that guerilla stuff, but Action Company is dependin' on us to hold this LZ for them to land here."

"Action isn't coming," said Waldo. "Once Chuckie hots up this LZ, no slick will dare land. We're on our own and we better think of ourselves first and now."

"Waldo's right," said Mars.

Harvey stared around him at his troops huddling in their bunkers, cutting new covering logs, digging in deeper. "Right or not, we got our orders. We're stickin'. Gimme that." He snatched the handset from Kansas City and called battalion. "We got us a real tight situation here. Recommend that if you don't figure to put in here what you promised, that you extract us asap, over. . . . Roger that. I got your orders. But it's real tight here and there ain't that much daylight left. We may not be able to keep this LZ cold much longer. Recommend you get us out or them in within thirty minutes, over. . . . Roger, out."

"What'd batt say?" demanded Mars.

"Told us to sit tight. Sar'n, plan us a bugout route. Pick a prospective laager somewhere north. If Action isn't in here by dusk, we're movin out. Chuck knows where we're at and he's gettin' himself some more 82s. Waldo, plan some fires along the route Mars picks and some D-Ts at the site. Mars, find something that looks good on the map with maybe rocks or rough ground so we hunker down without diggin' holes. I don't want our entrenching tools chunking all night tellin' Chuck where we're at. Georgie Bee, you got what's left of first plat and all the guys on the eastern half of the line. Find Pinball and tell him he's got the western perim."

With his dispositions made, Lieutenant Harvey led Kansas City, still shaking with short-timer's nerves, into the safety of the treeline. Together they squatted over a tin-can stove punched out of a C rat and used a bit of C-4 plastic explosive pinched off Harvey's five-pound bar to cook their first hot meal in twenty-two hours. It was 1800; dusk filled the horizon and the space between the trees.

A half hour later Chuck, uncertain that all the Yanks had been withdrawn on just three helicopters, probed the perimeter and took two wounded for his trouble. Harvey had to report that to batt; the slicks refused to come into a tiny jungle LZ that was hotting up, especially when there was a division and a half of gooks down there and absolutely no element of surprise. The pilots had the image of the downed chopper in their minds, too. The Batco went with the flyboys: The expenditure of another twenty-odd men (not counting the FO, who came from the artillery battalion and wouldn't be the Batco's responsibility if lost) was better than losing a string of choppers and all of Action Company. That was no way to get his Legion. Besides, he was infantry and he liked to watch the infantry fight. Night fell. Action never came. Harvey had lost the company's chance to escape by itself. Chuck began to probe the thin perimeter.

5

THIS IS HOW the night went: First, there was a stirring in the soul that seemed to each soldier either fear or courage but was both. Second, there was the screaming that never stopped. Third, there was the dying.

Georgie Bee on the eastern perimeter, with eight men in two-man foxholes and Sar'n Mars breathing down his neck, watched evening slide up and thought that if his failed suicide attempt had not shown him he would survive this war, he would be dying tonight. As evening darkened, the Bee sent a few men sliding out through the broken weed to set out the claymore mines, which look like Polaroid cameras but are full of ball bearings and plastique. He pulled his camouflaged poncho liner around his shoulders and shivered as he adjusted the bipod on his M16, setting it in the bunker's gunport. He shivered with exhaustion, the cold sweat soaking his fatigues, the evening chill, and no food. His fingers trembled; they trembled every fight. He wondered if they would always tremble. If back home in Burgerland sitting in McDonalds years away from the war raising a Coca-Cola to his mouth his hand would tremble so much he would spill it on his face—and, worse, if it would happen so often he would forget to notice. The moon tried to rise; he cursed it to blackness. No breeze—good! Lieutenant Harvey crawled into the bunker and passed Georgie

Bee and Mars the Starlight scope to survey the woods in its green electronic lens. "You don't see any goddamn rocket launchers, do you?" Harvey demanded.

"Nope," said the Bee, concentrating on the green view of the woods. "If they was out there, their sights would pick up this Starlight's radiation pretty quick."

"We gotta risk it," said Harvey. "This thing's about the only edge we got." He crawled out to finish his rounds of the foxholes.

The machine-gunner behind his M60 began to snore standing up. Bee was astonished and outraged; he jostled the gunner awake. In the pale fluorescence of the stars, the Bee under his poncho liner looked like a mound of earth. For an instant he felt unfindable and unkillable. He continued his preparations for the night calmly, as though he were back home in Colorado again, deer hunting. He thought about the woman in Denver, about lying between her warm thighs as autumn stiffened the grass and trees shed leaves as carelessly as that sexy woman shed her clothes. Would a woman stay faithful to a soldier gone to war? Would she still wear his ring when he got back? He laughed at the stupidity of his thoughts; he thought like a jukeboxful of sentimental songs. His fatigues were suddenly cold and he was surprised to find them drenched with sweat. Blood moved painfully through his cramped arms. His eyes ached with the effort of searching the unmoving forest for that slight jerk of motion that would betray Chuck.

"There they are!" Mars shouted. "Fire!" Claymores *whooshed* alive, their pellets gouging up earth. Machine guns, rifles, grenades—Chuck was gone! The forest was still again! Orange-red tracers zinged across the night. "Stop it, stop it! Cease fire!" shouted Mars.

Georgie Bee's heart pumped in his throat, his weapon smoked, the bitter stink of cordite gagged him. But he relaxed quickly, sliding back into the combat routine of watchful anxiety alternating with mindless terror. Again he began watching everything quietly, a trapped animal, brushing everything from his mind but a Chuck-scenting concentration. The trembling had left his hands.

Willard Mars crawled down the line to check for wounded and returned with the news that two of the Bee's men lay dazed and staring at the sky, their ears blasted from the concussion of their own mines placed too close to their position. They'd been too afraid of Chuck to string out their claymores the proper distance into the trees.

Green enemy tracers streaked level and flat from the forest. *Yellow blast of a grenade!* Tinkling fragments showering down, Bee's ears minutes behind his eyes, yellow still shrieking across his face, his ears ringing with the grenade burst, he squirming deeper into the earth, pulling his trigger in long bursts filling the black before his eyes with red fire, screaming, "Cease fire, cease fire!" and meaning it for Chuck, but his own men ceased firing and so had Chuck. Quiet. His finger snapped away from the trigger. His stomach and his chest lurched and he threw up out the gunport. He sucked a dozen fast breaths. He glanced over at Sar'n Mars: His face was caved in. The grenade had him. "Great God, Sar'n Mars, are you dead?" he cried. The machine-gunner gasped and fell back against the wall as Mars's corpse rolled backward with a wheeze that said, "Yessss."

Georgie Bee put a blank expression on his face and stared at the black night. He had no more thoughts of the woman in Denver. He picked up Mars's radio handset and called Harvey. "Mother Hen is dead," he reported.

Waldo carried many fears but his worst was the fear of mortars; it was natural for an artilleryman to fear most the weapons he used himself. Waldo listened for them as he ran across the tiny meadow; he knew they would be silent. He watched; he knew he would never see their muzzle flashes. His ear insisted it heard the distinct bangs of an 82! No, no,

no, that was crazy. But he expected to turn his head and
see yellow blasts! To feel pounds of steel clanging through
his skull! To jump and run and have his legs and arms
hacked away, his headless corpse gushing blood. He expected to see mortars burst once in unison and then work
quickly over their FOB in professional jumps, first out and
then in and away, following each running man into his
ravine and bush, scouring his ragged flesh, smashing at his
bones. He wanted to run, to scream, to cry for mercy. His
body lurched and shook. He searched for the yellow flashes
among the black trees. He pulled out his campknife to
defend himself and then he knew that he was going mad
with fear, that his fear would kill him. He stood in the
meadow and laughed like an idiot. He willed calm onto his
face; the effect seeped into his brain. He must be cool to
live. He did not struggle to be calm; he simply turned off his
brain. He refused to think. His body survived independently on its senses. He dived for the Bee's bunker. *A
yellow burst!* A crash like a door slamming in an empty
house! Grenade pieces blasted past his ears; Fruitcake's
M16 was shattered and torn from his grip.

He clapped the handset to his head and shouted over the
screaming of the new-wounded and the machine guns' roar,
"Firemission, firemission, firemission!" He was on his
knees screaming fire orders into the phone, red tracers
coursing away from the perimeter and green tracers zipping
up at him, he had only his knife in his hand, he was
hysterical.

"Target india, battery two, fire fire fire!" The terrain in
front of him expanded, glowing swooping outward, metal
and dirt and rocks spattering over the GIs, their rifles and
machine guns blasting long orange streaks into the yellow
light as they cheered and howled. He fell on his face
overjoyed.

"There! There! Over there! Watch my tracers!" Georgie

Bee shouted from his bunker and the line swung its weapons' fire onto three dark running figures.

"Running VC!" Waldo shouted into his radio. "Repeat! Repeat!" He grabbed up a grenade launcher he found lying there behind Georgie Bee's bunker. "Add five-zero, fire for effect!" he howled, and he loosed one round after another from the grenade launcher, snatching up snub-nosed grenades from bandoliers strewn on the ground, firing the next round before the previous had impacted, and there in the stark forest lit by the bursts of his grenades the artillery exploded again and he watched the Chucks throw out their arms and weapons and be swept away by cannon fire and by MG fire and their remains ground down by his last grenade.

He found himself on his knees again. He heard the screaming again. The last artillery bursts did not blot it out. The grenadier whose weapon he held lay face down on the bunker lid screaming into the ruptured sandbags. Waldo rolled him over and the screaming stopped as the man died. Green tracers crisscrossed in front of Waldo and he flung himself off the bunker and into the jumpdown hole, dragging with him two bandoliers of grenades he had stripped from the grenadier's corpse.

"Shout 'Comin' in' before you dive into a man's foxhole, Waldo, you scared the daylights outa me!" yelled the Bee's machine-gunner as he faced front to watch the silent black woods, the screams of Americans and Chucks echoing in the trees.

"We'll have Spooky on-station in an hour," said Waldo. "He's in a fight over in Pleiku right now."

"Lotta good that'll do us when we'll all be dead by then," said the Bee.

"What's your casualty count here?"

"Three, best I can tell, all wounded but still shooting. Sar'n Mars is dead."

"Dead grenadier on the roof of this bunker. I didn't see his face," said Waldo. "Take my 16 ammo." He unslung it and looped it over a stub of a log supporting the roof. He patted Mars on the shoulder. "That musta been fast."

"Didn't feel it," said Georgie Bee.

The machine-gunner stared resolutely into the trees. "Quiet now."

Another battery of defensive targets roared into the trees, raising to a high skittering screech the wails of the Chuck wounded out there.

"When it's quiet like this is a good time for me to check the line." Waldo crawled up out of the bunker and low-crawled north through the battle-littered stubble of grass to the next bunker. "This is Waldo up here," he said, remembering the machine-gunner's warning. "Who we got down there?"

"Waldo! We just about shot your tail off. Whistle or something next time you crawl around a man's position."

"Anybody hurt?"

"I'm Ayrab and I'm okay. We got an MG and it's okay, too. The Hardluck Kid's with me. He's in paralytic shock or something. He hates bunkers and we took a grenade on top. That did him."

"Don't know what to do for that. Here, take this—it's all I got." Waldo handed Ayrab a metal flask of vodka. "Don't get smashed. Ya got work to do." Waldo crawled away.

Ayrab took a fastidious first suck. He was hyper enough to drink it all without effect. He pried open the Kid's lips and forced the vodka down his throat, slapped him and gut-punched him, and the Kid came around. "Christ, it happened again, didn't it?" the Kid yelled.

"Nothing happened again. Drink some of this. It's officer's booze and it'll make ya big and strong. Drink. Waldo's orders."

The Kid drank and his eyes cleared. He said calmly, "Ya ever seen a rocket come into a bunker?"

"Naw, and I never want to."

The Hardluck Kid was Timothy Curry, Private First Class, assistant gunner on Ayrab's MG. He had a pale girlish face that made him look, when he went into one of his trances, like a marble child. Around his neck with his dog tags he wore a silver crucifix given him by his mother, but because silver sparkles in sunlight and moonlight he had wrapped it in black electrician's tape. He often worried that the tape covering might diminish the power of the cross. He wiped sweat from his trembling chin and rested his hand on the .30 MG as they both peered out over their assigned field of fire. "There was twelve of us in this bunker, see, and a couple of boom-boom girls," said the Kid. "It was a first-rate bunker, on Bridge 25, and one B40 come in. It went through eighteen inches of sandbagging like it woulda gone through windowglass. It went through three twelve-by-twelves holding up the roof and buried itself halfway through the sandbag wall on the other side. While it was doing all that, it threw off so much energy and sent things zapping around inside that it was like an egg-beater got in there. I was standin' in the doorway when it hit. It threw me down. I had the hard luck to survive. I got up and found all my buddies like goo, like someone had been smashing tomatoes on the walls. That's all that was left of 'em." He fingered the black-taped cross at his throat.

"Makes me wanta be sick," said Ayrab, staring out into the woods where the continual *KRUMP!* of the defensive arty fires continued.

"You were one of 'em who found the downed chopper, weren't ya? What were they like?" asked the Kid in morbid curiosity.

Ayrab glanced at his hands, which still seemed so ash-white to him. They were trembling again. He put them on the MG. "I really am gonna be sick if—" There was Chuck! "Those Mikes got satchel charges!" Ayrab clamped his finger on the MG trigger and cut them down.

"They got rockets! They got rockets!" screamed the Kid, scrambling for the exit.

"Naw, naw, naw! Just satchels!" Ayrab shouted over the clatter of his gun. An MG opening fire was the prime target Chuck's rocketmen were looking for. The B40 rocket went into the gunport whizzing past Ayrab's ear just as the Hardluck Kid scrambled out into open air. The bunker and Ayrab ballooned up out of the earth, carrying the Kid with them into the meadow, where he lay stunned, his back broken, his legs twisted at bad angles, until the fight was over and he died at last, free of his memories.

Waldo, at the north end of his eastern perimeter line in the last foxhole, leaped up, firing grenades into the breach left by Ayrab's MG and was astounded to find an enemy squad there rushing in—how did they get through his arty fires?—but they ran past him screaming like fear-maddened animals running from the continual hail of steel and then they were standing gawking around in the tiny meadow and a dozen rifles sent orange tracers crisscrossing through their bodies and they pitched over dead.

The last dead Chuck fell on Lieutenant Bad-Henry Harvey, lying in the meadow as the central point from which to use his Starlight scope to direct accurate rifle and grenade fire at the Chucks infiltrating through the woods. He wanted to avoid using his MGs because he didn't want Chuck rocketmen to know where they were. They were too valuable to lose. Harvey pushed off the groaning body and stuck his bowie knife into it and it shrieked as it died, unnerving him, and he stuck it again without thinking. "Chuck's bringin' in rockets!" he shouted to the line. "Keep a-watch!" He glanced down at his wristwatch's luminous dial strapped face down through the pen slit in his fatigue jacket: 0300. Mother! Dawn in two hours. This was going to be a near-won thing. He gazed around his base, the luminous glow of his watch dial burned into his vision. Would he ever forget all of this and, in his old age, remember only that moment peering in fright at his watch dial held three inches from his nose? A hell of a stupid thing to remember, he thought. But better than remembering Peepsite being torn to pieces there as he fell from the helicopter when the search teams returned. He lay there in the clatter and roar of the artillery fire coming in, the racketing of machine guns and grenades momentarily overwhelmed by the whooshing explosions of the arty, and dreamed of the future, but it was a warped future, a frightening future in which he found himself living a half-life of aspirin and orange juice, going to work in the truck tire retread shop (the only work he could find in the hard economic times before the war; the only work he would expect to find after the war) in a doped aspirin haze, sliding his hands around the rough bags as he tugged them over the big truck tires and lifted them into the cooking racks. He would go home, take out the gunstock oil and some old rags and rub the oil into the table-sized slab of black walnut he had in the living room of his rundown three-room house. In the kitchen he had the half-welded pieces of wrought iron for the table legs and his wife wanted them out of there. He would fill the rag with oil and run his hands over the sleek wood, rubbing in the oil, his tape deck playing quietly, his body cool and tight from his evening shower. He would spend the evening working on the wood and he would avoid thinking. His wife would watch him, as she always did before the war, from the doorway of the kitchen and be happy that he was calm, at least until the night took him when the torments of war that bubbled in his brain even now would be worse because he could not escape in the fury of combat. An odd escape. What troubled him now and what he knew would haunt him into the calm future was his knowledge that he had failed the men he was supposed to lead tonight. He had not bugged out when he had had the chance. Now they were trapped.

Harvey jumped to a crouch in the meadow, hauling his radio on his back and the Starlight on his M16 in his hand.

He had used the scope too long from one position and if Chuck had some Starlights of his own or even a good perceptive gunner on a B40 tube with Russian sights—and not the usual bamboo poles Chuck used for launching his rockets—then they'd have Bad's laager and range and they'd have him next. Harvey thought of that too late; that was his constant failure. Two heavy .30 Ak47 rifle rounds came zipping green at him. The first took him in the pelvis and he screamed as it spun him and he grabbed to see if he had any balls left as the second smashed into the radio on his back—the radio saved his life—and threw him forward into the soft earth as it burrowed into his back and stopped behind a lung. He lay screaming a long time before he realized he had only thought he was screaming—he hadn't the breath to scream, the pain was so great. Blessed shock flooded out of his system like dope, covering the pain and giving him the euphoria of the dying. He was thankful. "I'll never see my wife," he said to himself in his dying dream, and he passed out.

"Bad's got it!" came the piercing panicked wail.

"The company's bought it!" screamed Kansas City, standing over the body. "Where's Waldo? Who's left alive? Am I the only one?"

More artillery blasted down on faithful schedule. Waldo appeared out of the dusty murk on the meadow. "He's still living. Help me get him under cover, then pass the word I'm in charge and you tell Georgie Bee—wherever he is. Got it?"

"Yezzer!" They stripped the ruined radio from Harvey and found his second wound, dragged him to his command and control bunker and left him down there with their one rifleman-medic, Weldon Cobb, who looked like he'd just been born, he was that covered in blood, his hair and bushy mustache plastered to his skin with it.

"Pinball!" Waldo yelled over to the next bunker to the

grenadier corporal in there. "I'm the CO now! Check the line for wounded, for ammo, and head count, and get your butt back here to me in thirty secs!"

"Yo!" Little Pinball with speed made of terror scrambled out of his dugout to crawl down the line.

"We're all gonna die tonight," said Weldon Cobb out of his fat, blood-spattered face.

"Old soldiers don't die. They just fade away," said Waldo.

"We ain't old soldiers," said the medic as Waldo clapped his arty net handset to his head again and said, "Yonkers three-one, this two-four, we're buggin' outa here. All the blueleg oscars are dead or wounded and I'm in command. I don't talk to blue net anymore, just to you. Got that? Over."

"Bug out, you in command, got it, over!"

The drone of a slow-flying twin-engined C47 aircraft came down to them. It had twin gatling guns mounted in its sides and could put a bullet a second in each square foot of ground for enough acres to fill up Texas. "We got Spooky overhead," Waldo said into the radio. "You tell him to hose down these coordinates, and I'm givin 'em to you in shackle"—he fumbled through his mimeographed code-book to give the map coordinates—"and then tell him I want him to hose down everything between my laager here and those coordinates along azimuth four–six hundred, got it? Over. . . . Next, at my command fire all Delta Tangos simultaneously, over. . . . Next, at my command put steel on my location, over. . . . Right on, I said on my laager— we'll be gone when I call for it—don't argue, you ain't out here, over. . . . Forget the corpses, I'm gonna save live ones. Steel on my laager, out."

Pinball tumbled into the bunker dragging a captured satchel charge behind him. His shaggy brown hair was pasted to his scalp with sweat and mud.

"What's the bad news?"

"We got ten effectives, Waldo, on both sides of the perim, and six WIA, two of 'em can't walk."

"Cobb, get all wounded in the northern bunker. We bug out from there. Take two men to help you. You got ninety secs."

"Roger!" The medic dived out of the bunker into the rack and roar of the still incoming artillery fire, diving under the green flames of enemy tracers.

"Pinball, send one man to tell Georgie Bee we're buggin' out and to rally his men on the northern bunker in two minutes. You do the same. Move out." Pinball leaped up into the violent night and was gone.

Waldo spoke into his hand phone: "Yonkers three-one, two-four, bugout in five minutes. Tell Spooky to go to work. Fire all Delta Tangos, over."

"Spooky, Delta Tangos, out!"

Waldo stripped the unconscious Harvey of everything useful, looping Harvey's ammo bandoliers on top of the grenade bandoliers Waldo was wearing, and slinging his M79. He picked up Harvey's M16 with its starlight scope, slamming home a fresh thirty-round mag. He took from Harvey's pockets his hand grenades (he hated the things; they always went off by themselves), pulled their pins and rolled them out the gunport to explode in the confusion of the forest. "Dog tags!" he said aloud. "I forgot the tags!" He ran out of the bunker and in the moments left to him ran crouching over the men crawling to the assembly point and yanked the second tag from each corpse and pocketed it. Then he ran north across the meadow through a crazy warp of green tracer shouting into his mike, "All Delta Tangos azimuth four–six hundred cease fire! Spooky to move north, over!"

"Delta-tangos four–six hundred cease fire—Spooky north—roger, out!"

He fell on his knees with the Bravos huddled behind the northern bunker. "We got all the wounded?"

"Some of 'em are gonna die before we get a hundred yards, Waldo."

"Then we take their tags and leave 'em. Spooky's plowin' up a new laager for us. We follow his red fire and when he stops shooting, we're home. Got it? We leave no wounded. Got it?" The arty fire to the north broke abruptly and the black night there, clouded with smoke and dust, was suddenly still. "That's the yellow brick road. Georgie Bee, you're the tailgunner. Nobody fires unless I say so. We don't want Chuck to see us out there. Let's go!"

Waldo led out on the point with Harvey's 16 in one hand and his radio handset in the other. They stumbled into a gouged-up shattered world of choking dust and bitter cordite reek, the trees shorn of leaves and branches and standing stark, stripped white against the black sky and dust-clouded stars, the earth underfoot bleeding black water and full of jagged metal biting into their boots. Men stumbled and fell, lacerating hands, crippling knees; the wounded began to scream and Cobb, the medic, with no more morphine, gagged them, and they plunged on. Behind them enemy fire into their old base increased to a rolling roar. Chuck was suspicious: No orange tracer was coming back at him.

The Bravos crossed the cratered moonscape that had been Waldo's adjusting point for a defensive target—it was churned-over nightmare cleared in the heart of the forest—and followed the red rain of Spooky's gatling gun and the monotonous drone of his two engines. They stumbled on another few hundred meters and Waldo called for the northern Delta Tangos to be fired behind them to keep the base ringed in steel to keep Chuck out of it and to prevent his knowing the Bravos had escaped. But Chuck was a tough and wily fighter: A burst of green tracers rose up from the center of the meadow like Chuck raising his triumphant flag over their bunkers and the corpses of their buddies.

As the remnants of Bravo company pushed forward, Waldo dropped to one knee and called in: "Three-one, two-four; fire on our laagersite, over. . . . Yeah, yeah, we're all out. Just fire the thing, out."

More triumphant green tracer bursts arced up over the old base as Chucks crowded into the meadow to howl victory. Then the curtain of steel descended in a yellow whooshing roar just as Georgie Bee at the end of the column passed Waldo, who stood transfixed, watching the shells pulverize the meadow and the Chucks. Georgie Bee turned to stare beside him as the rest of the Bravos with their wounded ran toward the slopes of Old Baldy, where Spooky sprayed.

They burst out of the trees running upslope, gasping and stumbling, as the first brassy haze cracked open the night horizon. There in the east, leaping up black and sleek against the dawn, were six Cobra gunships and a long stick of slicks. They were going to get out!

Then they looked upslope to where Spooky's gatlings had cleared a highway of blackened, withered trees and stared into the eyes of the 95-Bravo Chuck Regiment, sliced through the middle by Spooky, true; but like good soldiers, they'd stood their ground to wait patiently for Bravo Company; wounded as they were, they were still more a regiment than Bravo was a company. And then Bravo realized that the now seemingly endless stick of slicks and gunships leaping up against the rising sun was not coming to save them but to bring a regiment of Yanks against this regiment of Chucks on the hill.

It was like the hand of the Chuck god sweeping the hillside clean. All the Bravos on the hillside were washed away in the single blazing roar of the enemy regiment. Waldo groveled in the dirt. Georgie Bee was flung flat by the wind-sucking hurricane blast of all the guns and lay on his back staring up into the brightening fresh day where the gunships in their squadrons pivoted, using the bodies of Bravo Company as their marker, and fired endless battering volleys into the Chuck regiment, wondering how many times a man had to die to be safely dead and out of that war. Then the enemy bullets found them.

Part II

6

GEORGIE BEE AND Waldo stood in the trees watching the dustoff choppers swoop down behind the curtain of steel provided by the Crocodile gunships and incoming artillery to pluck away the bodies of Bravo Company. "How many Bravos survived?" asked Waldo.

"None," said the Bee. "Only the lieutenant. He was so big and heavy it took those three guys to carry Baddie, and they took his bullets. Bad's alive."

"Yeah, in every disaster there's got to be one to go home to tell the story. Bad-Henry's it." Waldo looked away back to the south into the valley they had just left, toward where the ruins of the downed chopper lay, looking away from the racketing battle on the hillside where five battalions of paratroops were piling out of slicks behind their gunship protection and piling into Chuck. It was going to be a very big fight and it was going to win for everyone everything they wanted. Maybe even a front page article in *The Washington Post* to be passed from hand to hand in the Pentagon. Waldo adjusted his heavy load—the artillery net radio, Lieutenant Harvey's M16 with its precious scope, the M79 he had taken from the dead grenadier, and his multiple bandoliers of ammo and grenades—and turned downhill toward the valley. "Let's go," he said to the Bee. "We've got a downed chopper and one MIA to find."

The Bee adjusted his own misshapen pack of rats and ammo, threw the ute strap over his shoulder to hold the 16 at hip level, and stepped into the forest with Waldo. In minutes the clattering-*KRUMPING*-screaming-wailing battle on the hill was behind them and only the occasional ricochet sizzling through the treetops reminded them of it, and of the thirteen dead they had left on the slope, the twenty-six dead lying in their bunkers at the landing zone in the jungle, and Fruitcake, the country boy who wanted a medal, the first lost, on the civilized side of Old Baldy.

They tramped into a world where spirit and courage are not wasted. Through the green jungle canopy glittered diamonds of pale morning. A tawny brushbuck bolted across their path. The first bird of the new day stretched yellow wings and leaped cawing between the branches into the sky. They humped along in their field stink, their ragged filthy bloody fatigues, their smeared and half-bearded faces. They had been leaned by the steamy jungle marches and by the constant electric fear. Their minds had been honed to an unmovable singleness of purpose. They were traveling light. Pure soldiers now. The Department of Procurement's Vietnam War far behind them. The VC Valley ahead.

It was at 0600 hours with the forest already hotting up that Georgie Bee and Waldo, sticking under the canopy to avoid the air cav choppers and preferring to cut no trail but instead tramping an awkward route around trees and through brush, heard Fruitcake's ridiculous trademark chicken cluck. He had never learned to whistle.

"That's Fruity, ain't it?" said the Bee aloud. "We're Georgie Bee and Waldo. C'mon out."

Fruitcake unfolded his long body from the brush, a silly grin of delight creasing his dirty, pimpled face. "Well, well, where you been? Didn't think I'd see you guys again."

"Took us a while to catch up," said Waldo. "What's our disposition?"

Fruitcake's grin turned sheepish. He pulled off his bush hat and rubbed it over his crew cut, wiping off sweat. "Tell ya the truth, I've got myself a little bit separated from the company. Don't know where it is." He looked from Georgie Bee to Waldo. "Where ya goin', Lieutenant?"

"South. There's an MIA still out there, I can feel it. From the downed chopper."

Fruitcake licked his lips and adjusted the 16 on its ute strap over his shoulder. "You're a little bit crazy, ya know. Two guys strollin' through Chuckie's Valley by themselves."

"That's what we're doin'," said the Bee.

Fruitcake gazed off into the jungle. "Well, now. I got it in mind to catch up the company. I'm the best point man there is and they need me. I'll tag along with you two as we're all three headin' south. Three guns are better'n two." He smiled out of the grime on his face. "Ya wouldn't have any C rats, would ya, you could spare? I could use some 16 ammo, too."

Waldo pulled off a bandolier of ammunition and passed it over. "It's us three Musketeers, then. Ya figure we can put the fear of Uncle Sam into the 95-Bravo Chucks?"

"I figure we might," said Fruitcake, looping the bandolier over his neck and shoulder. "They ain't really seen American soldiers before. They got 'em a surprise comin'. I'll take the point." He led out loping into the brush.

Twenty centuries east below the morning sun and away from that piece of jungle where three lone soldiers tramped lay the immense American base camp outside the refugee hamlet of An Khe. Five thousand soldiers lived there, with beer, burgers, PX dollies, donut dollies, and plenty of fresh-mown grass for softball. Out of the base camp and straddling its perimeter line of machine-gun towers, stacks of concertina wire, landmines, and fifty-gal oil drums rigged with explosive charges, stood Hong Kong Mountain, honeycombed with Chuck tunnels dug there when the French held a small fortress on the same site, in which they built their pretty little lime green airport tower that now brought down on the Golfcourse transports and choppers. The Yanks owned the base camp; Chuck owned the mountain. Sometimes the Yanks would go up there and fight Chuck. Sometimes Chuck would come down off his mountain to blast away at the six base-camp 105mm howitzers manned by thirty gunbunnies who, because they were afraid of Chuck and had no confidence in the five thousand noncombat infantrymen with whom they shared base camp, had built their own barbed-wired, guntowered, mined perimeter within base camp. The peace of exhaustion, the peace of the five armies, prevented too much nastiness. Most afternoons, when the American clerks and the delighted-to-be-invited grunts who were R and R'ing in base camp took out their bats and balls and made up their games, Chuckie would sit on his mountain eating his fish-reeking muck and cheer on the teams.

Tanks patrolled the dusty roads through the weeds. Mamas and Papas in their jeeps mounting .30 MGs swung out through the tall weed looking for enemy infiltrators and Yankee deserters hiding in abandoned bunkers. Occasionally there would be a scare and a few companies of overweight clerks and cooks would be rousted out to sweep for landmines planted in the night. They would use their bayonets for that work, sticking them gently into the earth to feel for the metal, hoping there was nothing there to find. They were issued bayonets for that work; the field grunts had to steal whatever they carried into combat. The clerks all packed their wicked-looking bayonets in their freight and took them home for souvenirs.

Their nights were protected by startlingly bright lights from the guntowers, by long racketing machine-gun fire, and by the thumping and whooshing of the six base-camp howitzers. Each of the five thousand men in base camp had a weapon of some sort issued in his name—usually the obsolete M14 rifle with its .30 slugs. It was obsolete because it wasn't like the Flash Gordon little black plastic rifles: it was heavy and old-fashioned looking and made of wood, but you could throw the 14 against a tree, drag its action through the mud, never clean it and it would still be loyal to you and save your life, more than could be said of the 16. It took a good soldier to make a good rifle of the M16; she was a thoroughbred; she needed lots of tender care, plenty of gun oil, lots of clean rag, or she would forget to work just that one time you were staring brother Chuck in the face, him with his big heavy obsolete Nazi-invented, Russian-made, Chinese-copy Ak47 assault rifle. Five thousand men and five thousand weapons, and on any night 4,950 of them felt naked and afraid. The last 50 were the grateful grunts just in from the field too drunk or too heavily asleep to give a damn what came down off that mountain at them.

They were afraid, so they dug down under the central mound of the camp and there built DeeTOC, the Division Tactical Operations Center. There was no division there anymore; that had been the First Air Cav, the cowboys who had cleaned out this territory and made it safe for Saigon democracy. Their work done, they'd gone north. They left behind their hole in the ground, the red leather chair for the Great White Father—the commanding general William King—and a bunch of *Time* magazine clippings proving how great they were. No one made mention of the fact that the First Cav had lost its colors in Korea to the gooks and for that shame the army would not allow it back into Burgerland until the Cav had redeemed itself in blood. The Cav went at its redemption with a passion for newsclips.

In that hole within a hole, filled with desks made from old ammo crates painted gray, a cot on which was a rubber air mattress, plastic-covered maps pasted on the walls and littered with grease-pencil marks, and a dozen squawking radios, were a junior lieutenant and a senior sergeant. They were the Fire Support Coordination Center, charged with keeping friendlies from killing friendlies. The lieutenant had a routine of twelve hours' duty and twelve hours in the whorehouses of Sin City, something else left behind by the Cav; the NCO had a routine of twelve hours' duty and twelve hours at the gambling tables in the NCO club. They filled their spare time watching *Combat!* on television. The NCO was Staff Sergeant J. T. Raiby, a pale black, crew-cut, lazy man of thirty-two; the lieutenant, Second Lieutenant Edgar Engle, an intensely bored, freckled college dropout with buck teeth. "We're gettin' us some peculiar static outa the wrong place, Lieutenant," said Raiby, tuning the dial of one of their infantry net radios.

Engle set aside his copy of *True Man* magazine and perked up. "That static sounds like static to me."

"It's on the old Bravo Company freak, that's what it is," said Raiby, tuning closer.

They listened together, "Naw, just static. Probably all those choppers working out on the 95-Bravo VCs are drifting over on that freak."

Raiby shrugged, turned down the volume, and sat back, stretching one long arm for a mug of coffee, letting the static play itself out. They had a dozen radio nets to monitor—grunt, zoomie, Dragon, Crocodile, convoy, Hawkeye, armor—and there was always some freak static somewhere. Better static than some drunken ROK soldier getting on that net and singing "The Eyes of Texas Are Upon You" in gookish as they liked to do just when the Great White Father had all his Batcos in DeeTOC for a pep talk. Raiby listened absently to the static. It seemed to have some form but it was unidentifiable. Maybe it was some element far down south, their trans just trickling up. He stared across the radios into the bigger hole of which their FSC Center was just a wing, at the huge countdown clock no one ever used except to tell him when to go home, and at the starched-fatigue infantry officers with their bunker pallor, munching breakfast burgers and sneaking bourbon into their coffee. He had three kids and a wife at home, the kids pushing into the teens, and that cost plenty. He had his nightly game and could count on another few hundred in money orders going through the army mails to his wife tomorrow. He was a good steady breadwinner. If he extended his tour in that hole, pulling Sergeant First Class or maybe even Master Sergeant, Raiby could go home satisfied he'd done his best by his family in the war. He listened a moment more to the peculiar static out of the Bravo freak, and then put it out of his mind.

Georgie Bee tramped south through the valley with Waldo and Fruitcake. The short-timer's calendar sketched in pen on his faded camouflage helmet cover—the helmet swinging from his rucksack—showed he had six months in the war, an old-timer. But six months on a Burgerland clock is twenty years worth of campaigning in the jungle. He was an old man of eighteen. He was haggard, and the brightness in his eyes was not his fast-passing youth but alertness born of fear. He was exhausted from being spat upon by children, by ugly Montagnards, by whores; exhausted from seeing people forced to rummage through his garbage for food; from burnt-out homes, ruined fields, beer cans strewn everywhere; from counting the heaps of his mutilated enemies and of his mutilated buddies. He was a dog that had been kicked too often; he craved love but he was turning mean. Was he too far removed from the good man he had been before the war ever to find his way back? If a man is to live among his own kind he must cut his trail to the things in life that should be important to him—courage, love, friendship. But the Bee had no idea how to do that. No one had shown him the trail before the war and now he was lost in enemy territory. He was terrified.

A lifetime ago, he had wangled a pass into An Khe to get out of the field for a day's R and R and to be alone. Drinking black market Yankee beer bought from dusty roadside stalls along Highway 19 that cut through the ramshackle refugee hamlets, he wandered toward the brothels and steambaths of Sin City, looking in all the little roadside shop stalls as he walked along in the heat. He spotted a haggard old seamstress in a new stall—she may have been twenty-five for all he knew; Vietnamese women collapse from the delicate charm of adolescence to disastrous old age at twenty-five—and he looked in to see a naked baby playing under his grandmother's sewing machine. The seamstress looked up at him and smiled. She was a new refugee in An Khe, and she didn't yet hate GIs. It was a smile unlike those normally given to soldiers by merchants, bartenders, and whores; it was an ordinary smile, a decent smile. Bee stood in the hot sun and found himself suddenly smiling back at her, the first time in centuries he had done anything with his face except eat, drink, and gripe. He pulled off his cap and tromped into her shop. She seemed so incredibly small and ancient to him. Her skin was burnt to coffee and seemed to shimmer with life. Her long black hair was bundled in back and her eyes were of such a rich chocolate brown that he could not see the irises in them.

He sensed that she was frightened of him—this pale-faced, stooping, smiling, Occidental giant—so he sat down. He picked up the baby with a naturalness that surprised himself. It had been an immeasurable span of time since the Bee had wanted to hold a child. At the end of the day he returned to the war. That afternoon he spent with an old woman who had smiled at him and the baby was his single most vivid memory of Vietnam.

For Fruitcake in the lead of their little column, however, the war was a different matter. Like most soldiers he was a fatalist: Great uncomfortable events impinged on his life, things beyond his comprehension moved him where they would, and it was all he could do to dodge among all those forces to keep himself alive and marching. A soldier in combat is a natural animal with no past or future and only two choices—fight or flee. Fruitcake knew that. Mother Army had taught him that good lesson, and in doing so had made him a coward. It happened when Bravo Company met Waldo for the first time.

Waldo was then attached to Charlie Company of the mech infantry as forward observer, drank nothing that wasn't vodka and drank that all the time, had an instinct for directing steel, and was the FO every grunt company wanted because he was a cool Chuck-killer. Waldo's companies came out of the boonies whole; he kept the enemy at arm's length, pounding him with steel, saving grunt lives. He did it all himself—unlike other FOs, he permitted himself no recon team (no recon sergeant, no RTO) but chaperoned his companies alone, doing everything himself, including carrying that damn heavy Prick-ten radio with his fifty-pound ruck of rats and a little ammo for his .45. He wanted responsibility for no one but himself; he was prepared to sacrifice himself for his company but not ready to risk a recon team.

The Bravos learned to love Captain Daddy, to elevate Sar'n Mars to the level of myth, fearfully to respect B-2's battle mania, and to follow Lieutenant Bad-Henry because he was tough and usually right, but they were damned happy to see Waldo join them. But it had not started that way. First, the Bravos—imbued with the spirit of Mother Army—had had to save Waldo from himself.

When they first met Waldo at dawn on that bloody, torn piece of Highway 19 called Bridge 25, he was on his way to Long Binh Jail (LBJ). Waldo's own Batco was himself typing the stencil orders at that moment—for cowardice and desertion in the face of the enemy and for refusing the legal order of a superior officer.

That had been the 101st day in Waldo's war. Autumn leaves, autumn grass, eternal summer sky. He had blown away 10 million flowers that day with indiscriminate Harrassment and Interdiction Fire into the free-fire zone to keep Chucks off-balance. He was pulling the easy duty of temporary executive officer to the six-gun battery inside base camp (and inside its own fortified camp as well) while the regular XO took the cure for a busted leg. Waldo stretched along the warm sandbags of the main bunker, flexing arms and legs, dreaming of C-rat pizza and watching a heli lift from the Golfcourse, its defoliating guns retracted, enjoying the soft ease of base camp life as the summer sky faded to an insect-chirping evening.

"Alpha Rear, firemission!" barked from the radio in the command shack, and he and his bunnies ran to their stations as the jumble of words, names, numbers poured through the radio and the evening was begun, a long banging whistling evening supporting an infantry fight to the south, the howitzers banging out charge-7, the biggest load, making the hard-packed earth jump, raising thick clouds of dust, and bitter blue cordite that filled the fire base. The man who did not keep his hands clapped to his ears would go deaf. Even at that the blast of the six guns was like being slugged by a heavyweight champ with a pillow around his fist. The guns slammed out their rounds in bright sparking flashes against the black night, and Waldo could imagine the snub-nosed shells arcing up over the refugee town, then falling down into the jungle far beyond An Khe's eastern border and bursting in *whumps!* of spreading steel.

He went from gun to gun as the firemissions ran, one mission blending into another, inspecting the powder charges in each cannister to make certain that each was correct and that the shells would be thrown far enough and high enough to strike on target, neither short nor long. His reeking, buffeting, throbbing night suddenly showed palest salmon at the horizon; he was astonished that ten hours of war had passed so fast.

"Bring up the battery defense rounds," he ordered. "Use 'em up. They're getting old and stale." A gunbunny dived into a bunker, glad to get away from the ear-splitting migraine-making slams of the howitzers, and began hauling up the rounds kept specially prepared for short-range defense of the guns. Waldo inspected each as it appeared.

He turned from his inspection of the cannisters to watch the lay of the artillery flares he had been firing all night from the base piece and turned back to see the same gunbunny pass an old round to another GI who rammed it into the breach of his howitzer—a round unchecked by Waldo! Waldo jumped for the gun as the assistant gunner pulled the lanyard and the guncrew turned all eyes to their acting XO the instant the gun popped out the round—a charge-1 *pop!* instead of the deafening slam of the charge-7—and Waldo, rigid with terror, looked toward the town expecting to see the orange fan of steel burst there but he saw nothing. The round had cleared An Khe and fallen on its opposite side. He grabbed his charts and plotted the trajectory for a charge-1. He measured the lay of the gun. He recalculated. The round should have cleared all the outer eastern villages of the town. He picked up the radio and informed Fire Direction Control of his error. He continued to fire the mission for the troops engaged beyond the town. But through the last of night he called the troops in the jungle for confirmation of a short round. None came. No one reported friendly casualties. No one from the villages reported a short round. No one in the town reported an explosion. The guns banged over his head and he took a beating as bad as if he had been in a fistfight. The deep Asian night dragged on, the horizon that had once run salmon now seemed unwilling to welcome another day of combat with the thing in it that frightened Waldo. A dozen times he replotted the trajectory of the short round and could not believe that it had overshot the town. It might have gone into a house and been a dud and not exploded, but it would have gone through those poor wood and tin shacks like a tank. The fire base was fogged with smoke and dust and the taste of cordite. The heat of the guns roiled over him and he wandered the fire base with his .45 in his hand, loaded and cocked.

"My God, Lieutenant, you've got to put that pistol away," said the Chief of Smoke.

"It was a short round, Sarge," said Waldo.

"No one reports a short round."

"Then it was a dud. There's a village there. What if it took out a hootch?"

"More likely you center-punched a water buffalo. You haven't hurt anyone. We'll check it out after dawn. Holster that pistol."

"I might've killed someone—"

"This is war. People get killed. Why don't you put away that weapon until we see about things after light?"

"I'll keep it with me."

"So if we get a report you knocked down someone's hootch, what'll you do with that .45?"

Waldo went away into the smoke of the guns.

In the first of the red dawn, Waldo abandoned his post and went looking for the short round. He walked alone through the wire and napalm mines around base camp carrying only his pistol. He went alone through the jungle for a thousand meters and walked through two villages east of An Khe, following his plotted course across Highway 19 to a seamstress shop, through the silent crowd gathered there, into the shanty that no longer had a roof, into a room where he found an old woman and baby crushed beneath his hundred-pound dud projectile.

The morning minesweep tank found him alone walking west along Highway 19 toward the thousand French graves in the Mang Yang, his helmet lost, his .45 in his hand

dangling at his side, his blue eyes too wide and too bright.
They took him on with them because it was still Chuck's
country until the sun was fully over the horizon and the
minesweep patrol had checked the road. They took him
into the first fight of the day. Two B40 rockets crisscrossed
in front of the tank commander's nose and he fell back into
his M48 screaming but his driver, though unnerved, had the
presence of mind to turn the machine into the enemy
rockets, showing the toughest of its shell, and the gunner
fired one round beehive, the millions of tiny metal fle-
chettes shrieking through the tall grass where the enemy
lay. The tank took the third Chuck round neatly through its
soft underbelly as it ground down off the road onto the
shoulder, blowing fire through all its apertures and knocking Waldo from the tail where he had been clinging, the
heavy dying tank grinding over the enemy bodies pierced
through every square inch by the slashing tiny arrows.

When the grunt Batco came down with his choppers after
the fight was done and found Waldo there in torn fatigues,
streaked with tank grease, bandoliers of rifle ammo across
his chest, pistols under his web belt and a rifle in each hand
and the chopper radio screaming that SP-7 was under
attack, he took Waldo back up with him, shoving a grunt
Prick-ten at him and shouting at him to put it on redleg
freak and call fire for the strongpoint, and Waldo did. The
whole day went like that, choppering from fight to fight,
Waldo calling fire, moving from unit to unit along the road,
firing his rifles out of bunker loopholes, standing one-
handed on the backs of racing tanks with his radio handset
in the other hand clapped to his ear and mouth, scrambling
into choppers and out of choppers. He fought every fight
that day with every grunt unit on the road; he escorted both
convoys of the day; he called Phantoms for bombing runs;
he used Spooky's gatlings; and no one in his battalion knew
who he was or where he was because he refused to use his
call sign. A nameless voice came out of the battalion FDC

radio and the chart plotters knew that voice was the voice of battle and they went to work for it. He finished his day on Bridge 25.

He sat with the security force holding the bridge, eating the rats they gave him, drinking from the canteens they passed. Because they knew his reputation, they found vodka for him. But he did not speak to them, and they stopped trying to speak to him. Evening drew down. The last bright Lambretta three-wheeler full of chopped wood and the last cokegirl and the last bikeboy scuttled across the bridge for the eleven kilometer rush back to An Khe and safety. Chuck prowled in the night, but worse were the American artillery fires and the gunships that used all the countryside as a free-fire zone after dark, churning up the earth with steel searching for Chuck. Two tracks ground up onto the bridge, their weary troopers leaping off onto the asphalt for their chow, before the bridge guards dragged the barbed-wire barriers across the road at both ends, sealing the bridge. They went into their bunkers to do a little mild boozing and to listen to Hanoi Hannah. It was midnight of the same night when the Hardluck Kid almost stepped into the main bunker as it took a B40 round through eighteen inches of sandbagging and he staggered out covered with what looked like smashed tomatoes, wide-eyed and screaming. Again that nameless voice filtered into the stifling, dusty cramp of the battalion FDC in base camp and the howitzers began firing.

At LZ Schueller, eight klicks east of Bridge 25, Georgie Bee and Bravo Company were enjoying an evening's R and R out of the field, luxuriating in sleep in safe bunkers and eating good arty chow, when the alert gong rang shrill and the bunnies ran for their guns, and the crazy mech infantrymen clustering around their tracks began shouting, "The bridge! The bridge! Chuck is trying to blow the bridge!"

"Saddle up!" shouted the mech platoon leader, a lieutenant, his men already leaping atop their boxes, checking their weapons.

The artillery base commander ran out of his command post dragging on his shirt, saying, "Hey, hey! You can't go out there! We got standing orders not to let anyone outa this fire base after dark!"

"Chuckie may rule the night, buddy," said the mech lieutenant, "but that's half my plat on that bridge. He don't take them without takin' me." The track lurched forward, the mech grunts leaning into the wind, the brims of their bush hats pushed flat against the crowns, hugging their rifles and holding onto the gunshields.

Another track rushed up, empty but for gunner and driver. "We could use some help," said the gunner to Bad-Henry, and ten from Bravo swarmed onto the track and it ran out onto the black road, oblivious to landmines, Chuck ambushes, or the errors of the gunships swarming overhead. Even at eight klicks they could hear the larger bangs of the artillery crashing down and see the orange and green tracers arcing up from the bridge.

They roared down the road, two boxes, twenty men, all guns blazing into the night, and behind them—over the protests of the base commander—a Sherman of the Sixty-ninth Armored and one more track filled with Bravos came grumbling out of Schueller. They rode to the sound of the guns, like good cavalrymen, and they overran the bridge wire, firing like maniacs into the black night, scoring on the users of the green tracers, and here found the bridge blown to bits, the bunkers torn down, pieces of bods scattered everywhere, the Hardluck Kid stained red standing in the middle of it all spraying fire down into the small stream-bank, where Chucks screamed and flung satchels up on the bridge around him. They grabbed the kid off just before the asphalt was blown from a charge set beneath the bridge and the bridge ruptured, and it was then, there, in that, that the army taught Fruitcake the soldier's code. He was trembling and drooling with fright, his M16 and all his bandoliers empty, the bridge blowing up in his face, and he saw Waldo stagger out of a bunker that had just fallen in. The first relief tracks were stuffed with wounded and the track commander had flung his big box around and was ready to race back to Schueller, his own men peppered with bullets and two of them down in the track well sprawled on the ammo crates bleeding to death, the blazing dragon's roar of the approaching tank and track flashing at them from the darkness of the road east, the Chucks pouring in clever and heavy fire, and no one but Fruitcake saw Waldo there. Fruitcake bounded off the track before it sped away and dragged Waldo out of the dust. "Great God!" Fruitcake cried. "We're the only ones left alive on the bridge!" The first pair of relief tracks had disappeared into the night, guns empty of ammo, and the tank and third track with the Bravos had not yet stormed down to them, and there they were, stretched out on the fractured asphalt, no cover, Chuck bullets like a steel wall above them, satchels exploding around them. It was then Fruitcake determined never again to be in a fight. To keep away from the main body of men that must always suffer and die. To always take for himself the safety of the point man. He knew himself for a coward.

He dragged the stunned and barely conscious Waldo into a heap of ruptured sandbags and stuffed him down there among them, building a tomb of bags over him to protect him. He scrabbled along the bridge grabbing up dropped rifles, loose mags, stray cartridges, hand grenades, and flares and crawled back to Waldo's makeshift bunker and crawled in with him. The Chucks swarmed up onto the bridge as he knew they would; just before the tank arrived they would swarm away. But in that interim of thirty seconds they would kill him and Waldo if they could, they would rob all the bods, and they would turn Yankee weapons on Yankee soldiers when the tank arrived. He had to keep the Chucks away from him. He opened fire, and when he did, he drew fire from the enemy, a shattering screeching gut-turning, sandbag-bursting fire, and the coward wept with terror as he fired back. He scrambled from ruined emplacement to ruined emplacement, drawing their fire away from Waldo lying stunned among the bags, hurling his grenades. The Chucks were swarming over the bridge, running at him in loinclothes, bodies greased, bandoliers of Ak47 ammo crisscrossing their chests, some with satchel charges slung at their sides. They were firing from the hip as they ran toward him, surrounded him.

Suddenly the .50 fire from the tank's big machine gun was exploding on the asphalt of the bridge and the Chucks were leaping over the side into the water. Fruitcake with his long spider legs ran back to Waldo, all his ammo spent, all his grenades gone, only his bayonet in his hand, and then the tank was there beside him, GIs scrambling off its tail to grab him and Waldo and stretch them down on the tank's tail for safety. More GIs leaped off spraying fire; the big tank gun blasted huge gouts of yellow over their heads; they searched the bridge for the wounded, the dead, and the living, and then they were gone back into Chuck's night, steaming for Schueller, the gunships orbiting above the road pouring red streams into the riverbed. Waldo had come around and was crouching there, one hand clinging to the back of the tank turret, the other on the tank's radio handset, groggy but still calling accurate fire on the bridge, fused to burst overhead and scatter bits of slashing steel all over the bridge without harming the valuable road.

In less than fifteen minutes they were back at the fire base and saw that they had stormed out of the place without waiting for the barbed-wire barricades to be dragged back; the barricades were crushed. Fruitcake and Waldo jumped down off the tank.

Captain Foley, Sar'n Mars, and Lieutenant Henry Har-

vey stood there. "Give Waldo a drink," Harvey said to
Mars. The first of morning split the sky; they glanced up at
it surprised. Waldo wiped from his lips the bitterness of the
bourbon from Mars's canteen. Foley looked at Waldo like a
child who's just gotten the Christmas toy he always
wanted. Bravo could use a good FO. "We ain't got one.
You unattached now, Lieutenant?"

For Waldo those words were like being welcomed back
into the human race, forgiveness after killing an innocent
old woman and infant. Here he could be his own man, the
lord of fire of a dense and furious land. He bore the power
to save lives in exchange for the lives he had taken.

Fruitcake turned away from Waldo. The horrific battle
that had revealed Fruitcake's cowardice Fruitcake plainly
read in Waldo's face as the beginning of Waldo's self-
redemption. Fruitcake was a coward; he hated battle. He
knew he would turn and run if he could. But he also had had
imprinted on his soul his soldier's code, something he had
never known he had learned, and, despite his slinking
cowardice, the code would not let him abandon his company. He was one of them. They depended on him, as he on
them.

As for Waldo, what he did to welcome the morning made
him a Grunt For Life with Bravo Company. He picked up a
radio and called into his batt, using his proper call sign, to
report where he was. His battalion commander got on line,
hysterical with fury. "Get your ass in here!" the commander shouted, "I got a slot reserved for you in LBJ! You
abandoned your post in wartime!"

"That's right," said Waldo. "Tell the XO who busted his
leg he can have his six guns back. I'm humpin out with the
Bravos, over."

"Listen, you friggin' coward, this is a direct order—get
your tail in here, over."

"I had enough, Six. I'm humpin'. Your MPs can find me
in the Valley."

Waldo went out with the Bravos, and he stayed with them. It was Bravo's Batco Colonel Yoden who saved him from LBJ—good FOs were few and too easily killed (because they were overworked, spent too much time in combat), and Bravo Company needed him. Waldo's arty battalion commander tore up the stencil he had been typing and mused, with Yoden, that, after all, Waldo and Bravo Company might just pull down a couple of Silver Stars for their colonels, especially if there was some way to infiltrate them into the Valley where they could stir up a very nice little fight with Chuck. "We gotta look at things in the long term," said Yoden. "We take a little lip now, those guys get their blood up for it, and they'll do us a little fighting down in the Valley."

"Yeah," said the artillery colonel. "Then we get us some stars where it counts—on the shoulder, not the chest!"

7 ————————————————————————

AT MIDMORNING WITH the sun well up and their fatigues stained black with sweat, Fruitcake stopped just shy of a Chuck trail and signaled for the others to squat in the brush. They went down smoothly to one knee, their weapons ready, the brush around them not moving and their clothing not scraping it. They remained alert and unmoving for many minutes, their eyes moving in slow sweeps through the jungle, cutting it into sections, peering through the gentle breeze-drawn tug of leaves and the skittering motion of lizards on tree trunks, looking for that larger irregular motion that marked the movement of men.

Finally, Fruitcake loped uptrail, measuring the width of the enemy trail, looking for cast-off bits of equipment, torn fragments of cloth, and finding, instead, the marks still wet where men had stepped out of the column to urinate against trees. This was Chuck's valley and he moved boldly here, in big units carrying heavy packs and big weapons. He was not afraid here. Fruitcake squatted by the trail, listening into the south, and was satisfied that, despite the fresh urine marks, the column had moved quickly and was now far away. He slid back to the others. "How many you figure there are?" asked the Bee.

"Thirty to fifty, movin' fast," said Fruitcake. "From some blazes on tree branches, I'd say they've got them some 82s with them."

116

"Movin' south," said the Bee.

"Company must be down that way," said Fruitcake. "They're going after Bravo."

"We'll keep movin' south ourselves," Waldo said, "but we'll cut trail from here at right angles to this one, swing out west and then drop down. Wherever Bravo may be, we know that the guy from the downed chopper is down there and we wanta get to him before these Chucks do." He tuned his radio to the Bravo freak and spoke softly into it, trying to raise the company. "No go," he said at last. "Battery's weak or the mountains here won't let us commo." He tuned to the grunt battalion HQ freak and reported the enemy trail and direction but there was no reply. "We'll move out on skirmish line from now," said Waldo. "No machete work. We'll backtrack if we must but we leave no trail."

They moved out spread out abreast, five meters between them, each virtually lost to the others save for an alert hand signal, a cluck, or the sight of a black plastic rifle in the jungle greenery. They went due west, stepping over the enemy trail without disturbing its marks, and leaving no booby traps to raise questions in Chuck minds. They marched through the heat of the day when the birds, lizards, insects drowse in their treetops and the snakes crawl away into the mushy earth. They came to the edge of that piece of forest and drew back from the bright sunlight beyond. They chose a hard bit of ground with stones and fallen logs for a rest stop. Two drowsed against their packs while one watched. They ate what little they had that could be eaten without the noisy work of a P36 can opener. They lay motionless an hour and then were gone, slipped into the brush, their eyes sweeping the jungle ahead of them looking for the telltale marks of a man's passing or of a Chuck ambush waiting. In late afternoon birds and insects came alive with fury, *cawing* across the treetops, mosquitoes buzzing after them. The mosquitoes had their fill; none of the three would risk a slap nor would they smear on the mosquito repellent Chuck could smell.

In late afternoon, now moving south following the jungle toward the downed chopper, they again found the trail of the Chuck column, the urine marks still hot, the mushy earth of the fresh-made trail beginning to fill with water, and the jungle creatures just beginning to crawl out of the holes into which they had fled in alarm at the tramp of so many human feet. "Figure we're ten minutes behind 'em," said Waldo quietly, the blue eyes beneath the wild black hair searching the brush. "Trail's movin' out southeast now." He sketched the enemy route on his plastic map; Chuck was marching south but keeping well within the natural S-curve of the forest as it grew south from Old Baldy into the valley. Chuck was afraid of the gunships working out on the south side of Baldy and wanted to attract no attention.

The Bee measured with a finger the depth of a sandal print on the soft Chuck trail. He said softly, "I can't figure it. Why is this unit marchin' south, away from the fight up there? They ain't carryin' no wounded. These are all fresh men, heavily armed."

"It's the company," said Fruitcake. "They're goin' after Bravo."

Waldo quietly folded away the map. Cupping his hands around the handset and lying prone on the soft earth while the others searched the forest with their eyes, he called the grunt batt to report the change in direction of the trail.

Staff Sergeant J. T. Raiby, crew cut, his blackness gone flat and pale from too many days in the command bunker buried under the only hill in base camp, took the hamburger the buck-toothed and very-bored-with-the-war Second Lieutenant Edgar Engle handed him and shoved half of it into his mouth as he put his ear to his radio monitoring the grunt net. His eyes ran over the cards he had laid out practicing poker hands. He wiped ketchup from his lips with his hand and said to Engle, "We got any Lurps down south in the valley, Lieutenant?"

Engle, chomping on his own burger, his mouth bulging, shook his head. "Why?"

"I'm damned if there's not some commo still coming out of the valley."

"It's that business on Old Baldy, Sarge."

"Nope. Don't think so. This is the second trans to blueleg higher. First was garbled and weak, but this one was good and clear. Somebody down there calling himself Yonkers two-four reports a high-speed trail and thirty Chucks moving southeast."

Engle stopped chewing. "Can't be. Yonkers two-four is Second Lieutenant W. A. L. Daugherty and he's dead," he said around a mouthful of meat and onion. "Where's Meese. Hey, Captain Meese!" A thin infantry staff officer with an eighteen month bunker pallor looked up from his comic book. "We got anything at all down south in the valley? Lurps, Beanies, anything?"

"Naw. Everything's up on Baldy."

"Well, Cap, we got us an errant trans here, and it's a little weird," said Raiby.

The captain closed his comic book and walked across the concrete floor of the bunker, his white face paler under the fluorescent lighting. "Watcha got?"

"Sarge here thinks he's got Yonkers two-four on the grunt net," said Engle.

"Ain't poss," said Meese. He chewed his lip in thought. "We never got his body back, you know. Waldo, I mean. That's two-four."

"You think he could be out there two klicks farther south? We just monitored a report to your higher of a Chuck trail leading southeast."

"Naw. We lost one of ours, too, Georgie Bee. When you

don't extract 'em that first time, you don't get 'em at all. Tigers take 'em. What kinda trans was it—dustoff?"

"No, just the report of the trail."

"I oughta be gettin' that report from higher in due course, but I'll check with 'em now and see what they say. I bet it's just a freak freak comin' off Baldy, that's all."

Waldo, Fruitcake, and Georgie Bee stepped across the enemy trail and shrank away into the brush, dropping down to the earth in slow easy motions, their eyes searching the jungle to the limits the jungle permitted. There they squatted, barely within visual contact of each other, for many minutes. The trail was too fresh for chance taking. If Chuck thought he was followed, he would have left a bushwhacker behind him. More minutes passed and the jungle creatures frightened into their holes by the passing Chucks crawled out. The GIs slid away, disturbing little of the brush, avoiding as best they could the rasp of leaf on cloth, moving in a broad skirmish line. They humped like that through the late afternoon making another five hundred meters through moderate brush and heavy canopy. They had done well. As the first of dusk began gathering among the trees, they heard the snap of an enemy bipod connecting with an Ak47 barrel and they went to ground, sliding down to the damp earth like men being drained away into the mud. They waited, forcing breath to come softly and silently, and when there was no more sound, waited longer. At length they heard the chunk of an entrenching tool digging into earth, a man's laugh, a few words in rapidfire Viet, and caught the whiff of a small cook fire and roasting meat.

Waldo motioned to the east. They slipped separately into the brush and moved in slow, fluid motions around the enemy base, drawing back farther into the trees when the noise of work or the rattle of metal indicated a machine-gun position. They continued eastward until far from the sounds of the camp being dug in, until dusk had filled the spaces between the trees with haze, and the heat of the day had changed into a warm, mild evening, the sweat drying on their faces and backs. As evening quiet drew on, they drew together in the thin shelter of brush beneath a thick stand of trees.

"What do you think?" whispered Fruitcake. "Should we call fire on 'em?"

"Ain't no doubt they're Chucks," the Bee said softly. He rubbed a hand over his sun-freckled forehead, bursting dozens of tiny blisters, wiping their water on his fatigues.

"Yeah, we're gonna do that. What say I put a range and def spread on 'em and when I do we run southeast?"

"Might find that a bit of a problem," said Georgie. He removed his hand from the earth to show the tiger track into which he had put his hand. Eight inches across.

"That's a monster!" gasped Fruitcake.

"She's movin' southeast, where we wanta be."

"Everything's movin' south," said Waldo. "Everything's goin' after the downed chopper."

"The Chucks back there, they've got a little different idea from us, though," said the Bee. "I think they have it in mind to set up a bushwhack at the downed chopper and blow away anyone who comes down the valley on foot or in gunnies to extract that MIA."

"Yeah, they'd do that, the bastards," said Fruitcake. "It'd also draw the paratroops south and take pressure off the 95-Bravo Chucks on Old Baldy."

"That wouldn't be too good for our side," said the Bee. "The Chucks can cut Bravo's trail and know that Bravo is searching for the MIA but the Bravos won't know the Chucks are comin' down on 'em."

Fruitcake rubbed his inflamed mosquito wounds. "We gotta get south and find the company, that's all."

"Night in an hour," said Waldo, looking through the breaks in the overhead canopy. The birds had begun to settle into the treetops, chattering their evening greetings, nestling down for the night ahead. "All right. We call fire."

"Good!" whispered Fruitcake.

"We try again to raise the company by radio, too," said the Bee.

"Right. Then we run like hell southeast, we skirt the Chucks, and once we're in thick brush we sleep in the trees. Let's keep away from that tiger. First light, we move out again following the forest line south or southwest and we search for the chopper and for Bravo, whichever comes first. Right?" asked Waldo.

The others nodded. Waldo raised the handset to his mouth, stretched out on the ground again, and spoke quietly, calling for Bravo Company. No answer. He switched to the artillery frequency and called his batt FDC, gave his fire commands, and waited for confirmation.

"Lieutenant," said the FDC RTO with the harelip scar as he looked up from the radio that had just crackled with Waldo's fire commands, "what do ya make of that?"

The FD Officer stared across at the radio over the bottle of Coke he had at his sun-peeling lips. He put down the Coke, motioned toward a computer, and said, "Plot it."

"There, Lieutenant. Two-klicks-three south of Baldy, so it ain't nothin' to do with the paratroops," said the skinny computer man, setting aside his compass and ruler.

"What the hell could that be?" mused the lieutenant. "Answer him. Tell him to ID himself properly."

The RTO spoke into his mike and Waldo replied, his voice crackling out of the loudspeaker mounted on the FDC radio: "This is Yonkers two-four and this is a firemission, over." His voice was distant, thin, whispered, broken with static.

"Can't be," said the lieutenant. "Waldo's missing and that means dead." He sat in the oppressive dank of the bunker sloshing the Coca-Cola in its bottle, staring in mild confusion at the FDC radio that suddenly said, "Yonkers one-eight, this is two-four, do you hear me, over."

"Tell him we hear him," said the lieutenant. The RTO did. "Tell him to sit tight for five secs." The RTO did. The lieutenant cranked up the field telephone and put the handset to his ear. "Let me talk to Six," he said, his battalion commander. "Six, this is one-eight. Got a strange trans from two-point-three klicks south of Baldy. Someone ID'ing himself as two-four wants a range and def on a VC company. Right, he said 'two-four.' . . . No way to confirm, and we can't get a chopper down that way. They're all up on Baldy and you know those chopper boys—they won't leave a fight when they've the upper hand. . . . Shall I fire it? Roger." He put down the field phone. "Tell two-four or whoever it is we're going to drop a range and def spread on his target."

The computer gaped at the lieutenant. "You mean Six actually thinks it's Waldo out there?"

"No. But Six won't take any chances. Maybe there's a lost Lurp team down there. Besides, a target is a target."

"Or some Chuck with Waldo's code books and his radio," said the skinny computer grimly as he leaned over his plotting board, wiping sweat from his face, working his compass and ruler.

"Shoot it anyways," said the lieutenant. "Then we'll send some choppers down when we got some free and see what it's all about." The computers bent to their work at the plotting board, moving rapidly, and the RTO began to call fire commands to the guns at LZ Action in the west in the maw of the Mang Yang before battalion FDC turned over the mission to Action's FDC. Then the RTO called Waldo: "Two-four, this one-eight, we have your range and def coming in thirty secs, over."

"Roger," said Waldo. "We're movin' out, out."

They slipped away into the brush, moving quickly now to get far from the target area and stray rounds. They wanted to be a thousand meters distant but they were barely three hundred when the whistling overhead brought down the first artillery rounds and they went to ground, groveling in the soft earth, praying that that one-in-a-thousand short round didn't find them in their little piece of jungle.

"Call the air cav," said the lieutenant to the RTO. "Give 'em that laager. Tell 'em we want a sniffer down there right after dark. We wanta see if we killed anything more'n a few monkeys. Then we wanta see if a sniffership can smell Waldo or whoever the hell that is." He stared at the marks on the plotting board. "If he was alive, what would he be doing down that far?"

"If that's Waldo, he's exactly two-point-three klicks farther south than the last part of Bravo was when it walked into the 95-Bravo Chucks," said the skinny computer, tapping his grease pencil on the charts.

"What's he doin' down there?" said the RTO, running a self-conscious finger over his harelip.

"Whadya mean, 'he'? That ain't Waldo. It's somebody else."

The RTO turned to the skinny computer. "You just plot 'em, my boy, but I listen to 'em. I know every FO in this territory by their inflections and commo style. I'll reenlist if that ain't Waldo."

The computer blinked sweat from his eyes. "Then tell me, wise guy, why the bastard didn't run north like any sane man would instead of running south into that stinking valley?"

"He's down there, boy, I don't know why. He's down there and he's killing Chucks like he's supposed to do."

"You're both nuts," said the lieutenant. "Waldo's dead. I liked him and I wish he wasn't, but he is. Let's shoot this and then we'll go see who's using his call sign."

At the same time, in DeeTOC under its mound in the

center of base camp and three hundred meters from the redleg FDC bunker, Staff Sergeant J. T. Raiby glanced at the countdown clock and saw that he had barely another hour on duty before he could retire to the NCO club and his cards and a good, thick, red steak. He stretched back in his warp-legged metal chair and did a doodle on the action roster where he and Second Lieutenant Engle had kept track of all the action in the Area of Operations for the last twelve hours. It had been more than a busy day for him: Bravo Company had been wiped out, with two missing and presumed tiger meat, and only one survivor—their exec, the ex-ballplayer who'd never pitch again thanks to his arms and legs being shot full of holes and one nasty Ak47 round somewhere in his lungs, First Lieutenant Henry H. Harvey, now in a Qui Nhon hospital looking out on the white beaches and the Korean surfergirls, the lucky dog.

Waldo's voice came thinly through the redleg net to his FDC and Raiby froze. "Engle!" he shouted across the bunker. The lieutenant looked up in exasperation from his chess game with Captain Meese; it was the first time Raiby hadn't prefaced Engle's name with his rank. "Come listen to this! It's Bravo Company again!" Every head in the bunker snapped up. A dozen staff officers leaped up to crowd around Raiby's radios. The thin voice—whispered, in the jungle somewhere within earshot of the enemy, broken with static (a weak battery, no altitude for the antenna)—speaking in the deadly silent bunker with its fluorescent lights and its starched fatigue staff officers. "He's usin' the Bravo FO's call sign." They listened through the wait as the redleg FDC paused, evaluating what it was hearing, and they stared at each other in disbelief as the FDC announced it would fire the mission.

"They can't shoot that," said Engle. "There's nobody down there. This is a false trans."

Raiby sat in front of his bank of radios. "I been gettin' lots of strange static outa the Bravo net." He fine-tuned the radio to Bravo frequency. "Nothing now." He sat back in his metal chair, staring at the radio on which someone calling himself Yonkers two-four had just spoken, ignoring the staff officers clustered around. Raiby listened to the empty static coming out of the radio, and so did the officers, until they got bored, rubbed their clean-shaven chins or scratched their trimmed scalps and went back to their desks, keeping the countdown clock in view waiting for the shift to end. Raiby leaned forward to fine-tune the redleg net. Engle, still leaning over the back of Raiby's chair, said, "Whadya think, Sarge?"

"I think somebody's down there."

"Weird. He's smack in the wrong place to be. That's Chuckie's valley and once the fight on Baldy is over, every Chuck in the world is going to be streaming down there on top of him."

"Yeah, it's weird. A soldier in the wrong place at the wrong time, and he's trying to start his own war all by himself."

Over the crash and tear of the arty rounds gouging up the forest, Waldo, Georgie Bee, and Fruitcake could hear one clear rising scream, unchanged by the blasts of steel, climbing to that awful shrill like metal being torn. Then the range and deflection spread—a battery of six guns firing in unison over a checkerboard five hundred meters on a side, firing one column of squares at a time starting at the center and working out, then in, then out—moved on and the screaming stopped abruptly, leaving a hollow in the roar of exploding metal. After that a vast silence gripped the jungle. The attack was finished. There were no more sounds from the enemy position.

The three GIs got on their feet and moved quickly to the southeast as full night fell. They stalked through brush to a cluster of thick-trunked trees, ambushed the trees and the forest ahead for a long hour, the howls of wounded and dying Chucks coming to them only faintly and occasionally through the brush, blackness filling every part of the jungle and the night animals crawling out around them. They were too far from the ruined enemy base to know what was happening there, and they didn't want to know.

One by one, the other two guarding, they climbed up into the trees, each man in his own tree, putting themselves up far enough to be safe from tigers and deep enough in treetop foliage to avoid being spotted by Chuck Starlight scopes. They used their utility straps and pack straps to tie themselves in their trees, slinging their rifles from their necks, bracing themselves on heavy limbs, rubbing mud from their fatigues on their faces and hands for camouflage. They ate quickly and silently, listening deep into the jungle between chews, and fell into the sleep of the forest animals, a wakeful, watchful sleep. They woke together or in turns as night lizards skittered across branches, as owls hooted away from them in surprise to find them up there, as one lone cat—only the deep sound of its rasping breath identifiable to them from the dank blackness below them—prowled toward the ruined Chuck camp, as the yowls like babies' cries of other tigers echoed over the forest. Night insects bit at them, snakes passed them in the leaves, a startled tarantula dropped from the Bee's pack to the ground. Overhead a heli clattered, a slick with two doorgunners, and a second slick for shotgun. The sniffership was fitted with methane breathers; the human body gives off methane. It was searching for proof there were bods down in that charnel house of jungle the artillery had made of Chuck's base, and also searching for proof that the radio trans that brought on the devastation was made by a living, breathing Yank FO named Second Lieutenant W.A.L. Daughtery, out there in the jungle all by himself.

The sniffership clattered up into the black sky and went home. It had found proof that the arty expenditures had not been wasted; but it had not sniffed Waldo's scent through the thick forest canopy. The men in the treetops drowsed again. Late in the night, two great cats spat at one another, then shrieked in mutual outrage, waking all three soldiers, and they knew that the maneaters had found the Chuck camp. They slept. A single silent orange round, a ricochet, streaked up over the trees toward the waning moon. It woke all three of them. They knew then that Bravo Company, or some part of it, was truly down there south in the valley. They slept again, without snores, without movement, without dreams, the sleep of the forest.

At 4:00 AM the night had already proved a brilliant success for Staff Sergeant Raiby. At long last he had been promoted into the high stakes game in a back room of the NCO club, a game frequented by senior master sergeants, majors, and one hotshot second looey from the Twenty-fifth Infantry Lurps (the crazy Long Range Patrollers) who insisted on coming to each game with his shoulder holster over his camouflage fatigues. The majors, wary of the unpredictable Lurp reputation, insisted he hand over to them his pistol's magazine. The Lurp lieutenant sat there smiling boyishly around his stogie, irritating the majors and senior master sergeants as he raked in the heaps of dough, paid out in chips, in U.S. Green, and the Fu Manchu local stuff. But that night, his first in the big time, Raiby got the Lurp lieutenant's goat; Raiby started raking it in around 0200 and he kept at it until 0400, when the Lurp threw down his cards, spat out his stogie, begged the pardons of all the majors present, and stalked out of the NCO club, his pistol's magazine in his hand. Raiby had pulled in fifteen-hundred dollars in those two hours, and he could have done more but he was a shrewd and careful gambler who knew the limits of his luck. For him, gambling was like playing the stock market, an investment to make money for his family's future. He played, too, because he loved the game and the challenge and the threat, but he always quit ahead because he wanted this war to see him home in triumph, his bank accounts bulging.

It was a very French night in the highlands, he thought, cool and thick, full of mist, with fog up on Hong Kong Mountain sprawling out of base camp, the beacons of the radio relay station atop the mountain peering dismally down on the camp behind its barbed wire and guntowers. An occasional fine rain swept across the fields and Raiby stood in it feeling the cold tingling on his face, clearing his head of too much cigar smoke, beer, and hard concentration at five-card stud. It was his night for strange notions. That old mountain, the ancient village beyond the camp barricades, these wild roads and jungles and battered yellow people, the haunting memory of the French legionnaires who had once stood on this same piece of earth (and of their thousand graves on the west side of the Mang Yang). Standing there he could believe in eternity because it seemed to be all around him in the changeless earth and this endless war, in which he had a small part, small and safe enough to suit him.

The six-gun battery in base camp, barricaded behind its own loops of concertina wire, began to fire, their reports coming muffled—*POOF-BANG!*—in the mist. Another man came out of the club, his head snapping around first to the sound of the guns, so Raiby knew he was an artilleryman. The man unzipped his fly and urinated on the ground, saying to Raiby, whom he did not know, "I like this kinda night." He had the nasal tone of a repaired harelip.

"I do, too," Raiby replied. "I can sleep and there're no Chucks likely to come down off Hong Kong."

The man zipped up. "Night like this makes you wonder about things. Ya can't explain everything that happens in life, can ya?"

"Not hardly. Least of all here."

"Ya heard about Bravo Company?"

"Yeah."

"Well, I'm down there with the redleg, ya know, in the batt's FDC bunker. I'm the RTO. I know *all* our FOs by their voices. I should—I've listened to 'em all plenty." The man gazed up at the beacons peering down on the camp from the mountaintop.

"So?" asked Raiby uneasily.

"So I got a trans from one of our FOs who's dead."

Raiby looked around at the man. "Yeah? Who's that?"

"W.A.L. Daugherty. He was with Bravo. He's missin' now and presumed."

"What's your batt gonna do about it?"

The man shrugged. "We fired the mish he called for and in the AM we're sendin' out a chopper to looksee but no one really believes it's Waldo. 'Course, none of 'em in FDC or HQ have listened to Waldo over the radio as much as I have."

"You think it's him out there?"

"Sure it's him."

Raiby stared off over the perimeter, suddenly alive with the racketing of orange machine-gun fire as another crazy Lurp tower guard relieved his boredom. "Pardon me, I got me some work to do." He trudged up the DeeTOC hill and went into his bunker, the night shift surprised to see him. He stayed there the rest of the night, listening to the radios he fine-tuned to the redleg and the old Bravo freaks, drowsing sometimes and listening rapt other times as strange throbbing unindentifiable static crackled over the freaks.

Engle came in at 0600 on schedule and was astonished to find Raiby there. "You take this damn war too damn serious, Sarge."

"Could be," said Raiby, retuning the Bravo freak. "Could be."

8 ———————————————————————

WELL BEFORE DAWN the good soldiers of three units had rejoined the war. Waldo, Fruitcake, and the Bee had awakened and hung unmoving in their treetops until the first of predawn had barely colored the edges of the sky above the trees and issued a vaguely paler shade of night into the forest beneath them. In laborious and patient silence, moving with skill and grace, they slipped from the treetops, taking many minutes to bring themselves to the ground, choosing the places to put their feet long before they touched earth (like spacemen uncertain of alien soil), and then drifting away into the brush to squat and watch dawn come over the forest. This was the dangerous time, the worst part of a soldier's day, when ambush or stupid accident costs lives. They shrank back farther into the brush, wordlessly patrolling a circle of forest ten meters across until they were satisfied it was momentarily secure. With their hands, two guarding, each scooped a small hole to defecate, burying it with his hands. They moved away from there toward the southeast—toward where that orange American tracer had come from—on skirmish line, pausing at the moment the sun finally came fully over the horizon and into the trees. They shrank into the leaves, taking five minutes to open a can of food each and to eat and then to silently replace the empty tins in their packs,

131

and after five minutes, again wordlessly, using a minimum of handsigns, moving southeast after that startling moment of full flashing jungle dawn had passed.

As this happened, a second element of Chucks, another group of forty whose trail Waldo and the others had not crossed, edged out of their anxious forest hideout into the artillery-ruined Chuck forward operations base on which Waldo had called fire last night, and there found thirty-six men—eighteen KIA, ten WIA (all requiring hospitalization; it is far better to wound a man seriously than to kill him—a wounded man needs a lot of valuable resources to save his life and is a burden and hazard to his buddies who must see him to safety); eight only had survived, buried alive under heaps of dirt thrown up by the incoming batteries of artillery, the earth saving them from the flying chunks of steel that tore to bits their comrades.

The second Chuck element knew it had only the time between false dawn and true dawn to recon the FOB and to evac the wounded, that the American choppers would be there with the first full light to gloat over the dead. They swept across the base astounded at the churned-up, hopeless horror they saw: What the arty had not destroyed, the big cats had. They withdrew into the jungle with the ten wounded and the eight whole and the pieces of their dead. What could have brought on such destruction? This was no blind shot, no Harrassment and Interdiction fire. They had seen or heard no helis overhead except the one that had come over after the attack to sniff for the dying. Nor had they crossed the trail of any Yank unit this far south; Americans went in big groups with a lot of equipment and left big obvious trails. Their prey—Bravo Company, operating strangely alone and circled up in its base in the forest clearing—was too far south to have detected the unit here and to have called in the hand of the destroying artillery. No, they realized as they sped away from the ruin, searching the forest floor for signs, there was something else down here, another unit too small to detect easily, fast-moving, intelligent—Yankee guerillas! It must be the Lurps, the second element decided. Until they came upon the one mark left by Waldo and the others—the place where they had crouched beneath a stand of trees when Waldo had called fire on the Chuck base. Three men! Just three! The Chucks were astonished. Not even the Long Range Patrollers, all wild men, went in units of three. For the Lurps, five was a minimum and they preferred ten. For the short-range ambush patrol teams, fourteen at minimum, with three MGs and enough other weapons, grenades, mines to arm a Chuck company. Three men alone in Chuck's private valley? Absurd! But there it was, plain to see in the faint impressions in the soft jungle floor. Three men.

They worked quickly to bury the eighteen dead temporarily, or the parts of them that were recoverable. They did that to deny their enemies the advantage of knowing just how many the arty had killed. With the first churning of air overhead by the American choppers and the first flash of true dawn, they slipped away into denser forest to work their way west into the folded hills matted with brush and trees, well protected by heavy weapons and spider holes and a few antiaircraft MGs, to the underground field hospital of the NVA Yellow Division. Twenty men were sent on this duty with their leader's report of what had happened, and the unbelievable account of three Yankee guerillas operating independently in Chuck's private domain. The remaining twenty marched behind their young and curious captain, a man named Dong whose cheeks had been crushed by the concussion of a Yankee Phantom's bomb, his face scarred and smeared by that bomb and his ears melted and glued to the sides of his head. The weeks of shrieking pain that wound had caused him did not keep him out of a war where a professional of his caliber in a bitter war of attrition was too valuable to retire. That and his curiosity kept him in the war. The Yanks fascinated him:

What was the perversity in them that brought them 15,000 kilometers to fight a tiny war in a tiny country? Dong couldn't explain it. He hated the war, he hated the highlands, he craved his wife's fat body in the steamy south and he craved his old profession as enforcer for a minor lord. He led the remaining half of his company in a slow and careful sweep of the forest, keeping away from the ruined FOB and the hovering choppers, to search for the three men who had brought on that disaster.

In the moments before false dawn the chopper pilots at the great American base camp climbed into their machines and cranked on their engines, giving them the full thirty minutes warm-up the metal needed and rarely got. At false dawn, arty and grunt observers piled into the slicks and they rose leisurely into the cold morning sky, drifting west toward the Valley following the gray snake of Highway 19 below. With full dawn, the slicks and a heavy escort of Crocodiles climbed for altitude and hacked south, keeping well east of the forces on the south of Old Baldy blazing away at each other in their morning fury.

The choppers found the Chuck FOB buried under heaps of torn up trees and soggy earth. They hovered long enough for all the observers to manufacture a good body count estimate—there were no whole corpses but plenty of pieces, plenty of blood, and they mistook the marks where bodies had been dragged into the forest by tigers as the escapes of wounded men—and then they rose into the yellowing sky, each of them wondering who it was lost in this valley who had called the fire, and called it right.

Three GIs tramped through another hot day, skulking behind the thin protection of leaves to save them from the thing a soldier fears more than death: that zinging screaming piece of flung-out steel crashing through the skull that leaves a man to die in hours of suffocating in his own brains and blood and terror or, worse, leaves him to live a vegetable life in some VA hospital, poked, prodded, pitied. They moved with supreme care and skill; Chuck's bullets had long ago taught them to be good woodsmen, something they had not learned on the marching fields of their Burgerland training posts. The army had all the right ideas; it just didn't believe in applying them. American soldiers were trained as guerillas but never allowed to be guerillas. The army taught them to be independent in combat, to move quickly, to make careful, well-aimed riflefire, to use their initiative. But when the army put its well-trained soldiers into war, it wanted them to stick together, to move on command, to spray the jungle with machine-gun-like riflefire, and to do nothing that would upset the plans of higher, plans designed to get them all bemedalled and promoted and, most of them, home alive. The army didn't trust its soldiers. In fact, no one but the combat soldiers thought of the war as a total war in which tactics and strategy *had* to work. Only the lives of the combat soldiers were forfeit, and there were not many of them. Only the combat soldiers, away from army constraints, fought the war the way it was meant to be fought—the way Chuck had determined it must be fought. Three American guerillas tramped across the valley's floor, and Chuck did not like their eerie change of character.

After a twenty minute rest break for chow and guarded nap, Waldo and the others pushed on, and quickly came upon another trail, much lighter than the trail they had found the day before, the trail of a smaller unit. They crouched by the trail—it had not been cut through the forest but the unit had moved slithering around trees and obstacles, backtracking when it had to—and searched the forest with sweeps of their eyes, not moving their bodies for long minutes. At last the Bee crawled to the trail to check it out, and reported that he had found one print of a boot heel. "It's Yanks, that's sure," he said.

"Could it be Chucks with U.S. boots on?" asked Fruit-cake.

"Could be. But Chuck doesn't move that carefully in his

own valley. It was a GI element. I think it was part of Bravo. Try the radio again," said the Bee. Waldo did; no response. "They may not have a radio with 'em or it could be knocked out." He rubbed the growth on his face, wiped sweat from his forehead. "What do ya wanna do?"

"We move on skirmish line again," said Waldo. "Fruity, you take the right flank and keep contact with the trail. The Bee and I'll keep each other and you in sight. You lead us downtrail until the trail looks fresh, then we break off and move forward and hope to hell we can ID ourselves before Bravo blasts us."

Fruitcake and Georgie Bee nodded nervously and the three moved out. A kilometer behind them in the jungle the twenty Chucks led by the curious and melted-face Captain Dong also had come across the American trail and were surprised for the second time that morning. They had not expected any enemy units this far south, and now they discovered two tiny units moving further south toward the downed chopper through territory that, were the situations reversed, no Chuck in his right mind would traverse except at night in a heavy column well strung out for protection against Yank mortars and artillery.

When fear is constant, a soldier can then say he was afraid at a certain moment and mean that against the ground base of fright he was especially terrified. Except for first dawn, a soldier is only afraid in that way when he is approaching his own lines and his buddies don't know he's out there. That supreme terror was what Waldo and the others felt at the moment Fruitcake, with the sense of danger only a self-admitted coward can have, signaled them to sink into the brush. It was mid-afternoon, the sun burning through the thick canopy, their uniforms drenched with sweat. They took their time in crawling together, moving soundlessly, making no leaf tremble. "The unit we're followin' is up there, " whispered Fruitcake. "I can feel 'em."

They lay still, listening. Nothing. "No one but an Indian could be that quiet," said the Bee. "They know we're back here and they're waitin' on us."

"I bet they think we're Chuck," whispered Fruitcake, his voice trembling.

"They don't respond to radio contact," Waldo said, "so we've gotta move up on 'em."

Fruitcake wiped from his brow the salt sweat that could blind him. "I'll push ahead. I'm the point man and I got a feel for just where they are. You wait here for my signal."

Waldo and Georgie Bee stretched out prone; any bullets that Fruitcake might attract, they didn't want to share. Fruitcake crawled forward, moving slowly, slithering around branches that might give him away in movement, pausing for long minutes to catch his breath and listen ahead into the forest. He had low crawled twenty meters, his 16 being dragged by his side, when he heard the slight scratching movement of a man shifting position on the damp earth. He paused. No more sound. All right, he thought, this is it! "Fruitcake!" he cried, neither shouting it nor saying it too quick. There was no sound ahead of him, even the rasping of the jungle crickets disappeared. He said it again, this time stretching it out: "Frooootcaaake! This is Fruitcake here, Bravo! Talk to me!" Still no reply. This is really it! "All right, you guys, Fruitcake is gettin' to his feet. He's movin' slow and easy with his hands in the air. Don't shoot. This is Fruitcake here." He got slowly to his knees, raising his hands with his rifle over his head, and looked down into the gray eyes of the little squad corporal Myron Pinball Bagirov looking back at him over the sights of his shotgun. "Pinball! This is old Fruity here. Ya ain't gonna shoot me, are ya?"

Corporal Bagirov jerked his head. "C'mon in, Fruitcake,

and lower your voice." He dropped the shotgun, still keeping it trained in Fruitcake's general direction.

"I got the Bee and Waldo with me. They're back in the jungle a ways."

"Tell 'em to come in, too."

The country boy gave his chicken clucking signal, slowly lowering his arms and shifting his rifle to the crook of his right arm, standing elaborately casual there to prove to Bagirov—the only one of the American patrol he could see—that he wasn't the front for a Chuck attack. There were enough traitors in that war for that not to be an unreasonable fear. Waldo and the Bee got carefully to their feet and marched through the brush toward where Fruitcake was standing, leaving no tracks but making some noise so the patrol would know where they were and that they were coming in.

Pinball laughed softly, put down his shotgun, and stepped out of the shrubbery behind which he had hidden, grabbing Fruitcake, Waldo, and the Bee in turn, saying quietly, "Ya bastards! We'd never thought to see any of ya again. C'mon in!" He led into a heap of brush in which Mars and the medic SPEC/5 Weldon Cobb squatted with a ruined radio.

"Yeah, now I see why we couldn't raise you guys by radio," said Waldo.

"Well, the damned thing's okay, really, it just looks shot-up. But the battery took a round and spilled its juice, so we did a little transmitting last night trying to raise the company and got back nothin' but scratch."

"My radio's not much better," said Waldo. "Battery's about shot. How many guys you got here?" Waldo gazed around the forest floor. Some patches of fatigue were apparent here and there among the bushes.

"Thirteen including me, Lieutenant," said Mars. "I got 'em all spread out circle-style, within fingertip touch of each other. Learned that from the Nungs. Them Chink mercenaries know how to handle themselves in the forest."

"One good mortar round'd take you all," the Bee said.

"Yeah, if they could get a round through that double canopy overhead. Anyway, this was temp. We got the feeling about an hour ago we were bein' followed, so we settled in here to wait to see who was comin'. Glad it was you guys." Mars used a filthy army green handkerchief to wipe salt sweat from his drooping gray mustache and his dirty face.

"There's plenty of action in this valley today," said Fruitcake. "Chuck could still give us a nasty surprise before we find Bravo."

"We got ourselves a little bit separated from the company yesterday," said Mars. "I think the company is just about due south of us now. At least that's our route unless you guys have a better idea."

"None," said Waldo. "If we push south, we'll find the company and the downed chopper's MIA, and that's what counts."

"You see the fireworks last night?" asked Pinball.

"We caused some of 'em," said Fruitcake. "Waldo called fire on a Chuck company in the woods."

"Yeah, we heard that, too. We also heard south of us, and that's why we figure Bravo is down there—somebody had a nice little fight with Chuckie about 0300."

Waldo said, "Okay, we been at this laager too long already. Let's move out."

"Glad you guys found us," said Mars. "Every extra gun is a blessin' in Chuck's country." He gave a low whistle and a few heads peered at him through the brush; "We got Waldo back," he said, "and Bee and Fruitcake." Then Mars motioned south. There was a mild commotion in the shrubbery and this lost fragment of Bravo Company was on its feet, moving in two staggered skirmish lines through the jungle.

Behind them, the curious Captain Dong of the melted

face paused in his pursuit down the faint trail left by Mars's little patrol and thought about the evidence he had. A small patrol, about the size of a Short Range Ambush Patrol, was moving south; it had picked up or been rejoined by a three-man detachment—sixteen to seventeen to eighteen men total. Too many by far for his twenty man half-company to engage, especially since they were moving with a special care and style he had not witnessed before in Yankee soldiers. He shrank offtrail with his troops and pressed his radio handset to his mouth, calling his higher, checking on the locations of other Chuck and NVA units in the valley. He put down the handset. Every Chuck unit was up on the mountain the Yanks called Old Baldy, fighting the para-troops. There was precious little left down here in the valley. But higher was sending a company south, heavily armed, to follow the American patrol's trail. That meant the captain's support would catch up in about four hours, just at dusk. A dangerous time for units to meet but a good time to recon the enemy ahead and to decide what to do with the night. If the Yanks didn't find Dong first and call more artillery on him. He glanced up at the thick overhead canopy. That could hold out most mortar shells but not a hundred-pound artillery shell. He gave the handset to his RTO; they crept south.

The Deerslayer—so called because he had once mistaken and killed a brushbuck for a Chuck on an ambush patrol—advanced through the woods with his M16 in one hand and his blued bowie knife in the other and, just before dusk, found the ruins of last night's Bravo Company base. The rest of the patrol peeked at the remnants and drew back into the forest. Waldo came to the treeline with Corporal Pinball Bagirov and they studied the remains in long, careful sweeps of the eye. "Damn thing is probably booby-trapped," said Waldo.

"I don't see anything that looks unusual there," said

Pinball. "They had a fight last night but they kept company integrity. Then they shoved out south this morning and pushed in their bunkers. You can see they were pushed in and not rocketed."

"No sense in going out there to nose around, though," said Buck Sergeant Georgie Bee, coming up behind them. "Chuck has had this FOB all to himself all day. What I can't figure is if the company fought here last night, why did Chuck just let 'em walk out this AM?"

"Yeah," said Pinball. "And where's Chuckie now?"

"Down there," said Waldo, pointing south. "Between us and Bravo."

"What say we sweep around this FOB and try to pick up the company's trail? Or the Chucks?" asked the Bee. "Then we keep off those trails though we keep 'em in sight as we move south?"

"Right, that's what we'll do," Waldo said. "But we need some concentrated firepower ready right now just in case we find us a bushwhacker close by. We move out in columns of twos if the trees permit. We keep quiet. And we don't start any fights."

They swept around the abandoned Bravo base and found the forest deserted. At the southeast corner they found the marks where Bravo had penetrated the forest at first light and there, too, they found the sure signs that the Chucks had bitten off more than they could chew the night before—the forest floor was lacquered with blood now black on the soggy earth, the brush, the trunks of trees. Bravo had circled up and driven off the enemy and then stormed through whatever containment circle the enemy had thrown around the FOB and gone south. It had been a fast, bold, shocking maneuver, and it had worked. The trees for thirty meters into the forest were chopped and nicked from Bravo's running gunfight.

Deerslayer, more brown than black covered with mud, his mammoth bowie knife in his left hand, came up to

Waldo and the Bee and said, "I been over the ground, both sides, and I can count no more'n thirty Chucks were here last night."

"That's not enough," said Waldo. "Chuck wouldn't attack a company of Bravo's size—that's thirty-three men—with just thirty. I sure as hell wouldn't."

"That's what they did. They musta figured they'd hold Bravo here until they got reinforcements."

"This valley can supply Chucks like its got a production line for 'em," said the Bee, gazing around suddenly uneasy.

"Yeah. We gotta assume that not only are there Chucks between us and Bravo, but that they mighta spotted either your trail or the three of us," said Waldo. "It's time to start thinkin' that the enemy is on our trail right now."

" 'Slayer," said Mars, "I want you on our far right flank. You keep in contact with Bravo's trail and keep us goin' the right way. The rest of us will move out in two skirmish lines, staggered, and we'll follow your lead, got it?"

Deerslayer nodded, sliding his knife into the scabbard under his fatigue jacket to keep it dry, and went down the trail's shoulder into the brush. The rest of the patrol followed, spreading out quietly, moving quickly, M16s, M79s, automatic shotguns at the ready. They humped into the darkening dusk of early evening and still Bravo's trail did not warm up. They weren't going to catch up to the company before nightfall, and they wouldn't risk walking over Bravo's perimeter in the dark when their own buddies would shoot them down for Chucks. Waldo called a halt. They shrank under the leaves. "Eat'em," he whispered. "No smokes. No talk."

"Want us to dig in?" asked Pinball. "We gonna make this our FOB?"

"Nope," said Mars. "We're too small for that. Takes too much energy and makes too much noise."

Waldo added, "When we've got plenty of dusk, we'll get up on Bravo's trail and hump south fast. We'll put two point

men out front and some flank guards. When we got plenty
of evening around us, meaning you can just see your hand
in front of your face, we'll pull offtrail and ambush it.''

"Jesus!" said the Bee. "We only got the one machine gun
and just two claymores. We ambush with that?"

"We'll do the best we can. If somebody's followin' us or
followin' Bravo's trail, we'll blast 'em and then we'll run
due east and set up Nung-style. If we blast 'em once, they
won't follow us again tonight. That'll give us a breather
when we move out at dawn tomorrow.''

Behind them, Captain Dong and his half-company approached the ruins of Bravo's FOB of the night before as
heavy dusk settled around the torn earth. He knew the base
had been booby-trapped—that was SOP for both Yanks and
Chucks—and kept away from it, circling around the perimeter as had Waldo with Mars's patrol, checking for signs of
what had happened and why. He found enough evidence to
show that a Yankee patrol had moved off on Bravo Company's trail and then had disappeared into the forest,
whether east or west he could not tell in the gathering
gloom. That was something he didn't like either—the
Yanks usually set up elaborate night camps, the kind of
camps the Chucks would set up only in their valley. This
Yank patrol was full of guerillas, and there is nothing a
guerilla such as Dong likes fighting less than another guerilla. He squatted in the blood-stained earth at the entrance
Bravo had made into the forest and decided that the Americans, unlike the Chucks, wouldn't move at night. They
were no good at it. So the Yanks would be settled in
somewhere as usual, wasting the night, while Dong's half-
company would march. If he could push his unit another
two hours, settle in and throw out listening posts, he might
be able to catch up the patrol early the next day, look it
over, and decide what to do about it. But he had two more
worries—the company that was coming fast down the trail

behind him had not yet caught up. What if it came bumping into him at night and his troops either opened fire on it or the company's noise gave away Dong's position? Then the murderous Yank artillery fire would rain down on them as it had rained down on another unfortunate Chuck company the night before. Second, what became of the VC that had fought Bravo here last night? The marks showed that the unit was following the American company, but that it had been cut by a third—perhaps 20 men remained, total. If *that* unit was out there in the night, what would happen if Dong's half-company bumped into it? Grim thoughts, all. He liked none of them. But he would not waste the night; he had to make time over the patrol he was following. But he would be cautious. They moved south rapidly, following Bravo's trail.

Mars organized the ambush. He preferred the traditional L-type, eschewing the fancier Nung mercenary or U.S. Marine things that only work if the men in them have been trained together in long hours of drill to do just that one thing. Even though the L-type required three machine guns and they had only one. He put that one at the corner of the L facing uptrail toward the north. The short bend of the L ran perpendicularly from the Bravo trail and had four men in it, all facing toward last night's Bravo FOB and whatever might be following. The long arm of the L was laid parallel with the trail and about five meters from it in the forest among enough trees to give them overhead cover from mortars and some protection from any enemy small arms fire, but with plenty of clear fields of fire to pour steel into the kill zone on the trail itself. The long leg had nine men in it, including the machine gunner and his assistant gunner. Waldo, Mars, and Georgie Bee took up their own positions: Mars at the far end of the long arm of the L to better keep fire control of his men; the Bee on the left side of the MG on the small arm of the ambush near the trail where he could look both up- and downtrail to check on any approaching enemy; Waldo snuggled down prone under his camouflaged poncho liner, his M16 on its bipod in front of him, the M79 he had scrounged from the dead grenadier two nights before by his side, his campknife stabbed into the ground, his .45 under his belt in back. Although an L-type bush-whacker may seem to be off balance with all its emphasis on its own kill zone and no defense to the rear, the point of an ambush is surprise. If the enemy approaches from the wrong direction, the ambush lets him pass without molesta-tion, provided he doesn't notice the ambush. Once an ambush is blown and the kill zone full of corpses, the ambush team grabs its equipment and runs, keeping what little ammo remains for a last-ditch defensive circle battle, if it comes to that. It rarely does.

The patrol was exhausted. None of them had had much sleep in the last forty-eight hours. They had patrolled nonstop, kept alert through Chuckie's long night, and had little to eat. Waldo had them sleep two-in-three, huddling beneath their poncho liners and looking like mounds of earth among the trees. What was left of the moon rose and faded away. Waldo was careful with his use of Bad-Henry's Starlight scope mounted on his 16, knowing it put a glitter in the scope of any enemy Starlighter or anyone with a Russian-made B40 rocket launcher. They slept in their turns the heavy unmoving dreamless sleep of the ex-hausted. The point man of Dong's unit came up the trail, was up and past Georgie Bee before the Bee overcame his start and nudged the sleeping man next to him. The nudge was passed down the legs of the L and the men, who had slept propped up on elbows behind their weapons, put their fingers over triggers or palmed claymore mine firing pins. Those who had hand grenades clutched them in both hands ready to pull pins and throw. Grenades would be useless to them in thick jungle but ideal on that little scratch of trail.

Georgie Bee gazed uptrail and breathed, "Jee-zuz!" The

trail, straight for ten meters there, was black from side to
side with men. Two squads, he calculated. Exactly one
squad more than a fifteen-man ambush team could be
expected to attack. He gave the sign to the man next to him
to do nothing, and the sign was passed on. The GIs,
unmoving in sleep and unmoving in preparation for attack,
lay unmoving still as the curious captain's half-company
streamed past them down the trail.

Waldo waited a half hour, until he was certain that was
the only enemy element moving on this trail, then he
motioned for the men to quietly gather their gear and push
off for the defensive fighting site they had chosen on the
map, three hundred meters east. They went less
soundlessly than in daylight but they went without disturbing the night birds or the sleeping monkeys. They slinked
away from the Bravo trail and met together in a broad circle
in the forest beneath heavy canopy that would protect them
from mortars, and there they went to ground, lying prone
on their bellies behind their weapons, those men who had
claymores setting them out the required distance. Then
they stretched out their arms and slid back into the circle
until each man could touch the fingertips of the men adja-
cent. They lay like that through the night, every other man
sleeping, his buddies on each side waking him when their
turns came.

They expected an uneventful night; the only Chucks they
had anticipated were Dong's and he had passed them
without notice. But in the deepest of the night at that
moment when even the big cats fear to prowl for the
absolute unearthly depth of the jungle night, something was
moving and it woke them all. They lay rigidly alert, breathing softly, forcing themselves to keep it regular, lying there
behind their weapons. It was Chuck. The second enemy
unit, 95-Bravo VC, had assumed that Captain Dong had
cleared the way for it; after all, Dong was not attacked nor
did he attack, so the route must be clear. This unit moved

with skill through the night jungle, following a route parallel to Bravo's trail but well within the forest to avoid any snooping sniffer helis and not to risk accidentally bumping into Dong's outfit.

The Chucks drew up together and sprawled out tired on the ground as their leader used his radio to speak softly to Dong. This leader was a veteran captain of the 95-Bravo Viet Cong Regiment who had taken the political name Nguyen—as common in Vietnam as Smith in Burgerland—and he had political ambitions, brave ambitions for a Northerner hated for being a double-minority—he was a Catholic and his great-grandmother had been Chinese. He had compensated for that prejudice by moving to southern Vietnam where to be Catholic was normal and where the hated Chinese were far away. Now he was puzzled to find that Dong, another veteran blessed with or cursed with six years more experience in this valley than Nguyen, had moved so far south so fast without trouble. Nguyen was determined to close with Dong as much as he could before giving his men a few hours' sleep. It would need both of their understrength units to sweep the jungle for the patrol Dong was following, and it would need the help of the remnant of the company that Bravo had cut up the night before in order for them all together to attack Bravo. He gave the order; his men came to their feet and tramped south.

They were skillful night marchers but they made some noise. Their trucktire sandals betrayed them as true Chucks and not NVA regulars, and they marched straight through the American patrol spread out on the forest floor. None of the GIs moved as the VC stepped on the stocks of American rifles, and kicked past American ribs, forty Chucks putting their feet on American hands as the Yanks prayed, the forest gloom so thick and the American camouflage of cloth, dirt, and shrub so complete that all forty of them marched through the American patrol without realizing they had penetrated one of the units they had come to destroy. They trailed on south while the GIs gasped at their good fortune. The patrol stayed as it was throughout the remainder of the night; none of them could sleep despite their exhaustion. The baby cries of the jungle cats filled their ears.

9

AT 0600 LIEUTENANT ENGLE came clattering down the angled concrete steps into the DeeTOC bunker and into the blue-haze of the fluorescent lights, leaving the brightening morning outside. He had been in the war for five boring months and he had not yet seen full daylight. "Sergeant Raiby!" he exclaimed, stopping flat-footed and staring across the banks of radios at his NCO sitting there on his warp-legged metal chair, eyes red-rimmed, his black face ash gray with exhaustion, an ear cocked to the grunt net "You think you're pullin' twenty-four-hour duty now?"

Raiby glanced up from his concentration, irritated to be disturbed. "No, sir, I just can't get this Bravo thing outa my mind."

Engle clomped around to his favorite metal chair with a padded donut on the seat for his hemorrhoids. He threw down another stack of *True Man* magazines, his supplies for the day's twelve hours of duty. "How long you been here?" He glanced over the night log, saw that nothing special had happened—a few sniffer readings, Spooky worked out on Old Baldy to support the paras, another attack on Bridge 25 near Old Baldy (probably to try to draw Yank forces off the mountain and back onto the highway where Chuck thought they belonged), and a few small arms rounds taken on the base camp perimeter from the village

of An Khe, or more probably from Sin City where the girls
were entertaining the Chucks and overbeering them.

Raiby rubbed his stubble. "I been here since 0300, I
believe. Might I borrow that razor of yours, Lieutenant?"

"Sure, take it. You don't want the Batco trompin' in here
seein' you in a combat shave. He'll start gettin' ideas about
where you'd better fit in in his organization. Like out in the
field with the crawly things." He looked at Raiby in puzzle-
ment. "Hey, if you were here at 0300 last night, what
happened to your poker game?"

"I skipped it."

Engle gaped at his NCO. "Never heard of you skippin' a
game. What's got you so bugged about this Bravo thing,
anyways?"

Raiby stretched his shoulders stiff from hours hunched
near the radios listening to the two nets—the freak for
Bravo, the company that had been wiped out when the
Batco had used them for a decoy, and the freak for the
redleg. "Can't really say, sir." He glanced at the younger
man. A few years younger, yes, but the kid had been to
college and that seemed to make him younger still. "All
right, I'll tell you. It's something my dad said to me once
when I first enlisted. It's Old Army and they taught it to him
in the Big War. He said, 'Never stop anything you start and
never start anything you must stop.' I think I finally understand what the old man was saying," said Raiby. "I've this
odd feeling that Bravo Company out there had the Old
Army in it."

"Bravo's blown away. There is no Bravo."

"I know that. I do. And maybe it's just that I'm tired of
this war and so bored that I'll think up weird stuff to keep
my mind busy."

"Yeah, that's what I'm beginning to think. When's your
R and R?"

"Two months. I'm going to meet the wife in Honolulu."

Static crackled out of the Bravo net and Raiby hunched closer to the squawker.

"Yeah," said Engle, watching him, "I think you need it bad."

"Hey, look at this, Engle," said Captain Meese crossing the concrete floor. "Raiby, you, too, since you got it in your head that Bravo is still out there in the boonies." He flung a map on their desk, small red dots marked on it in grease pencil. "This is what Snoopy sniffed out last night. Look at it—almost three klicks south of where they should be, there was a bunch of Chucks in the forest, three groups of 'em, and be damned if they aren't moving off south, away from the fight on Baldy. What for?"

The second morning after Bravo's disaster on the south slope of Old Baldy, the patrol with Waldo and Mars in command and Fruitcake in the lead stirred to their crouch in the moments before false dawn. The forest was still enveloped in sleep and silence. They crouched unmoving during the seeping in of dawn among the trees, watching around them with sweeps of eyes. Then they were off, pushing south, silently, and went to ground again at the moment that true dawn flashed through the trees. They secured an area along the sandal-printed path of the Chuck forty-man company, breakfasted lightly and quickly, took their turns in the brush, watched for a while, and then pushed off south again, keeping each flank on the Chuck company's trail and the Bravo trail where Captain Dong with his twenty men had gone.

Below them in the valley, Dong's half-company and Captain Nguyen with his full-strength company finally linked up, amazed that neither of them had found the Yank patrol nor any sign of it. The realization struck them: They must have tramped past the patrol in the dark. They had walked through an American ambush—replete with enough firepower to stock a Chuck company—and the Yanks had not fired. What in the world were they up to? What kind of Yank unit was it? Farther south, they could hear the faint echoes of battle. Light machine guns and automatic rifles, a few grenades. The unit that had caught and fought with Bravo Company was mixing with Bravo again, a thing it should not do until it had been reinforced by the sixty men of the two captains' units. But what if Bravo Company had set a trap for the remnants of that company down south? A company-sized trap? The two officers gaped at each other: The damned Yanks were trying to out-Chuck the Chucks! Nguyen's company moved south toward the distant firing, knowing they would not arrive in time to help but only in time to pick up the wounded. They moved fast nonetheless. Behind them, Dong spread his half-company across the forest and followed at a slower pace, a powerful rearguard to screen against the sudden descent of Waldo's patrol. It would do no good to be caught between two American elements, especially when they acted as strangely as these two elements acted.

Farther north, the American patrol began to move away from its breakfast rest stop. Fruitcake took the point; Deerslayer and a grenadier with good eyes took the flanks. They moved in a column, rapidly, ready to bring tremendous fire to bear should they walk into a trap. There were too many Chucks in this piece of woods to move on skirmish line. They marched through the morning, while Waldo used his radio sparingly to try to raise Bravo Company far south of them but failed. Here, among these trees and hills stretching to the mountains that formed VC Valley, communication even with the powerful receivers back in base camp where the artillery FDC waited for their call was impossible. Waldo got nothing but static in reply to his calls and finally gave up. It was good to know that the Chucks in this part of the valley were likewise deaf. He listened for any choppers overhead or aircraft to whose freaks he might switch to use them for relays to base camp, but there was none. What was the point of sending anything flying this far south into the valley? It was Chuck's valley and no Yank would be down there.

They marched south, slithering around brush, using no machetes, leaving the barest trail—they were seasoned soldiers in enemy country. Weapons ready. There is only one useful thing about close-order drill and parade ground marches: They make a soldier feel like a soldier. Now these soldiers tramped in their sweaty torn dirty fatigues, their makeshift equipment and packs slung on their shoulders patched and torn, the fighting weapons in their hands grimy and speckled with rust because they'd not had time to clean them properly, but as they tramped they felt like soldiers on parade. There is nothing so grand as being in the middle of a body of men in uniform and parading in blocks of units across a flat grass field beneath your guidons and flags and a pure blue sky, your rifles and bayonets flashing: You feel part of something powerful, and indeed you are. You feel that you can tramp through vast desolations and terrors and tramp to the edge of the earth and back so long as those flags flutter and the cadence count rings true. They marched that way into the depths of the valley, feeling grand, powerful, unbeatable. Nothing could turn them back, they were sure: They were the grand Chuck-killing army of the republic.

They moved under lighter canopy where the forest had thinned and a man could see twenty feet instead of just five, where the forest floor was crawling with grab-your-ankle vines, wait-a-minutes, come-alongs, and the birds in the treetops, unalarmed by the silently passing patrol, chittered at them glad for the company. The two Chuck units ahead had made no effort during the night to leave no trail; they were easily followed. At high noon the patrol came upon the place where the two units had joined, paused for breakfast (leaving their own tins and wrappers in the brush, carelessly hidden), and moved south. The American patrol had not heard the gunfire from Bravo's morning fight but it was obvious now that the combined Chuck force ahead of them was going down after the company. But again the Chucks, too confident in their own territory, had left plenty of signs of their intentions: The main body had gone south rapidly in column while a smaller group had spread out to march south more slowly, screening the main column's rear from whatever might come down the valley. Odd that Chuckie was being so cautious in his own valley. That could only mean that he thought something was following him. They started off southward into the forest and knew that they could not go in there carelessly. A Chuck element was there as a rearguard and it may have set up a bush-whacker. At the least the Chucks would have planted mines.

Waldo, Mars, and the Bee crouched under the brush as the patrol spread out around them and sank down out of sight. Waldo unfolded his plastic map. "We get into some rough country ahead. Hills, folded ground. Good place for Chuck to ambush. We wanta try to flank 'em before we get there. Look at this—we got this little mountain here to the southeast. It's got plenty of tree cover over the crest—"

"Says the map," said the Bee.

"That's all we got to go on." said Mars. "Seems to me these Chucks are stickin' to the valley because they expect Bravo to stick to the valley, like we always do. Let's go up this mountain and down, march fast, and that'll put us either ahead of Chuck or on his flank; either would be good."

"Yeah," the Bee said. "It could also dump us smack between the two Chuck elements."

"It can do that."

"I don't see any other choice," said Waldo. "I don't wanta walk through the forest after Chuckie has had time in there to set mines. We'll cut trail away from Chuck right now and go over the mountain."

Fruitcake led out with Deerslayer as the right flank guard to report when they had finally broken contact with the Chuck trail. The trail curved south-southwest. They moved quickly, worrying less about making sound or leaving tracks, but avoiding machete work—machetes ring like good new bells in a valley.

The mountain was 180 meters high, barely a foothill anywhere else in the world. Its lower half was thick with new-growth trees all rising up straight and true, with little underbrush. It was easy climbing, full of switchbacks; Fruitcake found the fastest paths. The heat of the day became intense but they were in the cool of the trees. They found a swift-running little stream of crisp cold water, drank their fill, and rested under the trees by the peaceful stream. Some men lolled back against their packs to drowse while others sat quietly staring into the forest, their eyes that had been strained from watching so many days and nights now cooled and refreshed with splashes of stream water. Mosquitoes buzzed; fire ants tramped in columns across the trail.

"Let's go," said Waldo, and they got to their feet and climbed higher.

They came to the military crest of the mountain after just two hours labor and found that, despite the map's promise, it was barren but for waist-high elephant grass. The American maps were thirty years old, modeled on poorly drawn French charts, and unreliable. "We move east," Waldo said. "We keep in the treeline and we go east around this crest, then down the south slope." They headed east, moving swiftly now, abandoning the effort to make no noise or leave no trail because this unplanned extra piece of march was going to cost them too much time. They did not want to spend another night out of Bravo's protecting perimeter.

They found the eastern slope even more barren than the crest: The mountain slid away to the east and southeast through thick elephant grass and boulders, and beyond its slope lay a panorama of all of Vietnam—the rugged wrinkled mountains leading to the haze of An Khe on the horizon, beyond that the sparkle of light from the glass windows of the vehicles zipping through the American base camp sixteen klicks distant, and the pale blue bowl of sky overhead. The land was yellow, green, brown, cut with snaking blue black rivers, filled with slapping-bright, insect-buzzing jungle reeking of rotten nuts and animal droppings and infiltrated by yellow vipers, and by forests like back home, forests with needle-strewn floors, tall, straight brown tree trunks, and birds chirping from the limbs. They went quickly around the mountain into the open, quietly, with apprehension: Chuck could see them too easily, but they had to risk it to make time.

The slope was far steeper then they had expected. Fruitcake cut a narrow trail barely eight inches wide and they moved along that, the steep slope of the mountain breaking away beneath them. They moved crouched against the face of the slope, grabbing bits of grass or plant roots to hold themselves to the mountain's face, their heavy packs and weapons threatening to drag them down into a boulder-bouncing roll into the fields below.

They plunged into young forest on the south side with relief, breathing heavily not from exertion but from fright. They regrouped and moved downslope, angling to the southwest now, and came across the second branch of the little stream that they had crossed coming up. Here the stream burst from the mountainside in many places but had not run in volume to make a clear flow. Here it drained downslope in a long, curving alley of mud. The soldiers, footsore and hungry for rest, jumped onto the mudslide and slid down the mountain, following the stream's curves around trees and roots and boulders, lying back on their packs to slow themselves and stretching out their legs for speed, slipping down in silent, wordless, childish delight.

The mudslide dropped them near the valley floor in a

place where the draining water had encouraged a marsh, elephant ear plants growing big enough to hide a man standing and the marks of slithering vipers easy to see. They sank their canvas boots into the muck and grimly marched south searching for higher ground, putting their feet on whatever was firmest to leave the least trail. Lizards and dark brown frogs skittered from their path. A cool breeze blew in their faces. The pale yellow brown sky of late afternoon shown over them. Fruitcake's cluck was sharp and clear to them here where the birds no longer *cawed* but whistled, and they went to ground. He came back to report. "Stove-in FOB up ahead, Waldo. Looks like it ain't been used in a couple years. Plenty of growth on it."

"We'll skirt it then," said Waldo. "You lead out, Fruity, but watch for traps and mines."

They marched in column around the ruined base. It had the look of a Chuck encampment, particularly the shape of the circular mortar pits, and it had no plastic-woven sand-bag cover on the overhead logs but sod instead. This had been a big Chuck effort; he had built it for a big fight here in the valley in the old days. They stared at it in curiosity, wondering who Chuck had fought then.

"Hey, hey!" said Deerslayer on the right flank. He had picked it up automatically and now stood startled at what he held in his hand.

Waldo motioned the column to earth, then approached Deerslayer in a crouch. "That's a mine, 'Slayer."

"I know it. A souvenir of the U.S. Air Force. Can I put it down?"

"You better. Slow." They studied it where it lay on the mushy earth. "Been out here a long while and it's a dud," said Waldo. He and Deerslayer surveyed the ground. "Whole area must be mined." After that battle in which Chuck had used these bunkers, the Air Force had strewn some of its many toys across this piece of valley. It was a weapon suited for comic books: Cannisters of aerial mines were dropped to burst open and shower down hundreds of packages that, once the wings had flung open, looked like winged golfballs. The mines glided to earth, struck hard ground, then bounced up into the air head-high and exploded. A wonderful weapon that had no value against men in bunkers. Of course, there was always a percentage of failures—mines that refused to jump up after striking soft earth. Those the Air Force was pleased to leave behind in the valley, a quick way to mine a large area in a free-fire zone. Unfortunately, most of those mined areas were never properly recorded on operations maps and many American units walked into them.

Mars said, "This could be a blessing. We know Chuck won't come over this way, so if we cut west from here and then head south, we can pretty much count on our left flank being secure for a time. We'll do that." They marched away from the bunkers and out of the mined area, moving with excessive care and very little speed. They cut south-southwest looking for the Chuck trail and the marks showing that Bravo Company was down that way. They moved with silent speed, fearing that they might have gambled too much—they could stumble into Chuck or he into them or they could run into Bravo unprepared. The results would be the same.

As evening began to close around them, the captains, Dong and Nguyen, brought their units together to discuss what had happened. They had lost all track of the American patrol and that worried them. Either the patrol had flanked them to join Bravo in the south or the patrol had another mission and had gone out east or west. In any case, they had lost contact and they had to report it to higher; higher would be furious. That meant they had to close with the wounded Chuck company in the south that was keeping contact with Bravo and see what kind of a party they could put on in the night to assuage higher's anger over their losing the patrol. Their sixty men plus the twenty-odd leftovers of the wounded company should be enough to overwhelm thirty-three Americans whose ammo had to be running low and who, oddly enough, had called for no Spookies, gunnies, or zoomies in the last two days since the fight on Baldy had started. They moved south in column with point, tail, and flank guards out, not worried about leaving trail; it was their valley, after all.

"Hey, Raiby," said Engle, "it's 1800, man. Let's get outa this hole and forget the war."

Raiby rubbed his red eyes. "I believe I'll stick around a bit, Lieutenant."

The night shift came in, its lieutenant saying, "Suit yaself, Rabies. In fact, why don't you hold the fort while we grab some chow from the Airborne Club. Ya want something?"

"Yeah, burger, and fries and Coke."

"Ya got it." The night lieutenant left.

"You aren't gonna stay here all night, are ya?" asked Engle.

"Naw, just a little while longer." Raiby glanced at the radio he had kept tuned to the defunct Bravo freak.

"You know there's nothing going to come out of that radio tonight. We got nothing all day but some static. Like I told you, it was probably just some leakage from the paratroopers' freaks on Baldy."

"Probably," said Raiby, tapping a grease pencil on the map he had spread out before him on the desk.

"Well, suit yourself," Engle said, shrugging. "See you in the AM." He left.

Raiby called across to the starched infantry staff officer trading his duty for his own night shift. "Hey, Captain

160

Meese. What say we put a redhaze down there in the valley?"

"To look for Bravo?"

"You never know what we might find."

Meese stared past Raiby at the huge wall map on which they had greased in what little evidence they had that something that wasn't Chuck seemed to be moving through the valley. The most impressive mark was the artillery fire that had been called in the night before on a Chuck company. It had been an accurate firemission, and a company of men had been destroyed, according to official body count. "Yeah, why not?" said Meese, turning to his replacement, a first lieutenant, to give him the instructions.

Raiby had his burger and fries and sat through the first part of the night with the night shift, listening to the crackle from the radios. At 2000 the results of the redhaze were in, the chopper boys wondering why any mission had to be flown that early when everyone knew that Chuckie didn't settle in until after midnight. Midnight for the redhaze—a quick flyover with sensors that could detect camp-fire heat—and then call in your arty asap just as old Chuck is curling up in his blankets for a peaceful night in his valley.

The first lieutenant brought the marked-up redhaze chart to Raiby. "Meese says you're interested in this, Sarge. Here ya go." He dumped the map on Raiby's desk. Raiby clutched it up and stared at it. "There's a little something down there, all right," said the lieutenant. "But not enough to fire another range and deflection spread. If you want to put some H and I in there, though, you've got my approval. There aren't any grunt units down that far." He went back to his desk and the crossword puzzle he was working.

Raiby studied the chart. The redhaze had produced enough readings to show a peculiar semicircle of very small camp fires in the forest—about what a GI would build in a tin can to cook some rats. But it was a very un-GI setup. It looked Chuck, like a Chuck unit worried about taking hits from two sides at once and no time to dig in. That kind of

FOB made no sense unless Bravo was down there. And Bravo wasn't supposed to be anywhere.

He put down the map and rubbed his tired eyes. He had been with this strange thing so many hours—days now, days following a company that he knew had been blown away!—that he was no longer sure he was sharp enough or perhaps sane enough to really analyze what the redhaze showed. He looked again at the map. All it showed was some stupid gooks doing something stupid, which was what gooks did best when they weren't killing Americans. If he missed another evening's poker he could lose another three hundred dollars and lose his seat. He had heard nothing intelligible on the radios in the last forty-eight hours, and perhaps what he had heard in the beginning was, after all, just imagination. He slapped shut the map, got up, said to the night shift, "See you guys tomorrow," and went up out of the bunker, stretching his arms and legs and arching his tired back to get the cold bunker cramps out of them. He went to his hideyhole to get his gambling money and then down to the NCO club.

Four hours later and $127 ahead, Raiby turned up the last card on the dead man's hand—aces and eights, the hand Wild Bill Hickok held at the moment he was shot in the back. Raiby hated that hand; he hated seeing a thing another man had seen at the moment he died. He laid the cards face down and folded out of the game to the beery shouts of protest from the other players. He went out into the black cool night and lit a cigarette, feeling a mild breeze drift through his sweaty fatigues. His mind turned to Bravo Company; it was always with Bravo. He trudged up the hill to DeeTOC, clomped down the concrete steps into the fluorescent haze, and found twenty men staring wide-eyed at his radios. The night shift lieutenant turned to him and said, "God damn, Rabies, someone's fightin' a war down in the valley and no one's supposed to be there!"

At 2100, when Staff Sergeant J.T. Raiby was picking up

his first card of the evening and the full blackness of the jungle night had not yet been relieved by the fluorescent horizon of a silver moon, Fruitcake and SPEC/4 Robert M. Lefever, with his bassethound face and the shotgun he despised because he was terrified of its indiscriminate spray of lead, went quietly onto their bellies in the trail muck as the distant muffled roar of an ambush came to them from far downtrail. "I'd say that's a klick south," said Fruitcake.

"About right," said Lefever. A spray of mixed orange and green ricochets darted beyond the treetops. "Bravo."

Waldo and Mars sprang into the mud beside them. "Ya see anything?" demanded Mars.

"Naw. That's a klick farther down," said Lefever.

"Then it ain't the unit we're followin'," said Fruitcake. "That sandal print we spotted was still dry—no time for it to fill with water. They can't be more'n fifteen minutes away from us while that firin' is a good hour's march."

"It's Bravo," said Mars. "They've ambushed the unit that was followin' 'em."

"Or could be the other way around," said Waldo. He dumped his pack and rifle and, with only his radio on his back, shinnied up the thickest tree at hand. From its top, he could see nothing but black mats of leaves and black sky occasionally streaked with a silent ricochet. He talked into his mike: "Pagan four-six, four-six, this Yonkers two-four, two-four, how do you hear me, over."

Crackles of static. Then the excited voice of Kansas City: "This is four-niner, two-four, never hoped to hear your voice again! Six wants your laager—in the clear, over."

"Estimate one klick due north your laager if you're the boys doing the work tonight, over."

Captain Foley's voice came on line, the racketing of MG fire nearly drowning it out: "Your battery's weak, two-four. Ya got contact with higher or no, over."

"You're our first contact in two days, four-six. Give us your sitrep and we'll be down to help, over."

"Sitrep—we bushwhacked twenty Victor-Charlie doggin' our trail and we're pullin' out right now. What's yours, over."

"We're doggin' estimate fifty VC/NVA forty-five minutes max away from you comin' down due north on your old trail. Ya got mortars, over?"

"Rog, mortars. Thanks for the fifty, old buddy. Don't follow me. Do this—call steel if ya can, then bug out. Ya got a map, over?"

"Rog, map."

"Look at it. If I'm Houston and you're Chi-town, then you'll find a big clearing about Albuquerque. We'll meet there, over."

Houston, Chicago, Albuquerque! What kind of map directions were those? Waldo wanted to shout in frustration. They were the only kind Captain Oliver T. Foley could think of on the spur of the moment. Waldo peered at the map he held against his nose, his legs wrapped around the broad tree limb on which he sat, and, nearly smothering the light in the palm of his hand, gazed at the map in the thin beam emitted by his penlight, and found Albuquerque. A clearing was the wrong place to go and Daddy was no map reader but in the midnight jungle full of trigger-happy Chucks no place was safe and any hideyhole was good if it meant joining forces and putting the company back to full strength. "Roger, wilco, over," said Waldo.

"Good, two-four. Call steel and move out now. I'll give you sixty seconds before I drop mortars and run myself, out."

"Roger, out." Waldo flipped over to the arty net and strained his whispered voice into the mike and was about to give up—despite his treetop elevation and less radio traffic at night, the surrounding mountains were gutting his radio commo out of the valley—when a voice burst in his ear saying, "Station calling Yonkers three-one, we can barely hear you, over."

"Three-one, this two-four, two-four, two-four, firemission, over."

"Station calling three-one, I say again, we can barely read, over."

"Two-four, two-four, two-four, firemission, over."

"This three-one. Roger, station, firemission. What is your call sign and laager, over."

"Yonkers two-four, Yonkers two-four. Laager in clear is"—he fought with his map and the tell-tale penlight and spoke the coordinates into the mike.

"Roger, station. We have your laager as . . ." The voice faded. The battery, unused in forty-eight hours, had consumed just enough revitalized energy to report the useless stuff. Waldo drove his fist into the tree trunk in frustration. His sixty seconds granted by Captain Foley were slipping away.

"This three-one. Attention station calling three-one. Say again your firemission, over."

Waldo clapped the mouthpiece to his lips, speaking as clearly and slowly as possible and as loudly as he dared, knowing voices travel deadly distances at night. "This Yonkers two-four, two-four, firemission, fifty Victor-Charlie, battery-6 on this laager"—again he studied his map in the pale, concealed ray of light from the penlight in his cupped hand.

"Roger, station, I have your firemission at"—and FDC repeated the coordinates—"dangerously close to your own laager. Explain and ID yourself, over."

"Three-one, two-four, we're buggin' out asaper. Fire when ready, over."

The radio crackled with fresh urgency: "Two-four! Did you say 'two-four,' over."

"Roger, three-one, this two-four, over."

"There is no two-four. You the same two-four who called an R and D two nights ago, over?" The voice trailed to nothing. The battery was dead. There was nothing to do but hope FDC had enough of the trans to shoot. Waldo shinnied down the tree and found Georgie Bee. "Get Sar'n Mars and the boys," he said to the Bee. "We gotta run for it. Daddy's down south and he's buggin' out due west. He ambushed the unit trailin' him." The sudden muted *BANGS!* of Bravo's light 60mm mortars cracked over the trees in the blackness to the south. "He's droppin' steel on the forest to cover us. Plus redleg might be here—*here*—in sixty."

They collected the patrol and ran, heedless of noise or trail, running toward a thinning of brush beyond which glowed the fluorescence of horizon cut by mountains.

Noise travels great distances at night, and fifteen minutes below the American patrol the combined units of Dong and Nguyen, on a swift, stealthy, wary plunge south to support the twenty men Foley had ambushed, heard the patrol's clattering bugout and thought they were being attacked by the American patrol they had been trailing and had lost. They threw themselves down in a circle to open fire in all directions, their green tracers thudding into trees and ricocheting off stone. Foley's light mortars burst yellow up in the treetops and showered them with frags. They groveled in the mud in a black jungle night in the valley that had once been their private preserve. But the clattering of the patrol's hasty bugout saved Chuck lives because the combined units were prone when, three minutes later, the double-racketing, sound-barrier-busting, hideous shriek of American eight-inch howitzer shells came down through the canopy into the spongy earth and tore the forest to bits, men screaming themselves deaf, men flung in pieces into the treetops, sections of steel and stone and spears of tree limbs *whinging,* clattering into the blackness, suddenly erupting yellow, skewering shell-shocked men who were on their feet and running madly as their saner comrades groveled in the steaming shell holes full of jagged bits of thigh-tearing metal. And then it was over. Waldo had called for a battery-6—six guns, six times; FDC had given him its only battery of two eight-inch howitzers—the only guns available to range that far into the valley—but had had the guns fire eighteen times apiece over a modest deflection spread equal to a battery front of six 105s. In the howling, shrieking stillness that followed the two Chuck captains dragged themselves whimpering to their feet, smeared the mud from their faces and—to hell with secure silence—roared at those of their men who could move to clamber to their feet and run east, into the deeper jungle along the base of the stream-cut hills where the jungle canopy was thicker and the earth even softer and more able to absorb more Yank incoming. They ran fear-maddened, losing equipment and wounded and, once sloshed into a safer place, dug in with their bare hands. The two captains were astonished to count only twelve lost of their combined force of sixty. Of the forty-eight with them, two were wounded; which meant they could count on six more wounded straggling in over the night. They reported only six KIA to higher and when higher wanted a better explanation of the debacle, the captains decided the better part of PR was silence, pretended their radio battery was failing, and clicked off. They lay there the night in the snake-slithering muck waiting for the next Yank barrage to tear them all to bits, wondering what kind of Yank unit they were trailing, men around them moaning from the pain of the concussions they had suffered, the night eerie and terrifying. Late at night the realization came to them: Nungs! Of course! Chinese mercenaries in American uniforms and equipment. Who else? They hated fighting the Chinks—the mercenaries were animals who took no prisoners, used knives too much, traveled at night and never slept—but that, at least, was a rational explanation they could accept for the weird behavior of this enemy unit. They settled down to wait for predawn, snuggling in their slime, no one sleeping, hallucinating another artillery attack.

In the fluorescent DeeTOC the infantry Batco, Colonel Peter I. Yoden—burly like a football player gone to seed, his close-cropped hair gray, his thick mustache trimmed to within a millimeter of regulation width, his eyes red and yellow with too much concentration on his paperwork—was astounded at the lunacy that was suddenly hitting him from all sides. He recoiled from the redleg net Staff Sergeant Raiby had just tuned to catch Waldo's whispered trans to FDC, windmilled through the crowd of his suddenly superstitious and imbecilic staff officers, and grabbed a landline, cranking the bells of artillery battalion FDC, "Did you just tell somebody you're gonna shoot that mission?" he cried into the phone.

"That's right," came the young voice at the other end of the staticky line.

"On whose authority?"

"My own. I'm the FDO here and it's my job. Who'm I talkin' to?"

"Blueleg Six, who do you think? Gimme your six, kid."

"My six gave me standing orders to shoot whatever two-four might call in, sir. I'm doing it."

"I don't believe that. That's ridiculous. There is no two-four—he got blown away with my Bravo Company."

"Choppers never found his bod, sir, and someone using that call sign and sounding very much like two-four did call in a picture-perfect mission on a Chuck company two nights ago. My six says to shoot for two-four."

"I'll talk to your six anyway, kid. Put him on."

"Can't sir, he's not here. He's at LZ Action tonight supervising nightfire on Old Baldy for the paras."

"Where's your exec, then?"

"Blown away. I'm it tonight."

"A lieutenant?" croaked Yoden.

"Captain, sir."

"From the Point, I hope."

"Roger. Five years ago."

"Then you must be a good man. Listen to me and be sensible. You can't fire that mission—"

"Is there any blueleg down there I don't have on my charts, sir?"

"None. You know Raiby's too good to let that happen."

"Then I'll shoot it."

"Listen, man, you want to sacrifice the Point and a majority for one stupid mistake? That's what's happening here, you know—I'll burn you so bad in a private memo to the commanding general that no efficiency report your six can write on you—even if you six was Westmoreland himself—will save your career!"

The voice at the other end said quietly, "I've got no career, sir. I've got six weeks more in this stinking war and when that's over, I'm out of your army. This wasn't the U.S. Army *I* wanted to join. It was another U.S. Army."

"You mean you're sacrificing the Point—the Point makes a man a general!—for what?"

The line was silent in the Batco's ear. Then the voice said, "Do you know what 'shot, out' means, sir?"

"I do."

"Then: shot, out."

"You didn't just fire that target?"

"We did."

Yoden slammed down the handset. "They fired it," he said incredulously. His staff officers cheered until he glared them down. His eyes fell on Raiby for the first time since he'd been called out of his ranch-style bungalow built on the DeeTOC hill to witness the strange hissings from a radio call sign that was supposed to be dead. "Raiby, what the hell are you doing here?"

"Couldn't sleep, Colonel."

"Raiby, you get a goddamn air photo recon mission down there at first light. I want to prove to you idiots that a little static and some bleeding over from other freaks doesn't prove one dumb redleg FO is really alive and down there fighting the war all by himself."

"Yes, sir."

The Colonel stomped out.

10

Bravo Company and Waldo's patrol ran out of the forest exploding in orange and black, beelining without noise security for the clearing called Albuquerque. If they hadn't been expecting each other, they would have opened fire on each other. Instead, after thirty minutes of panicked stumbling, with chunks of arty steel shrieking overhead to thunk into trees around them, they joined up and then they all collapsed together in a gasping tangle of waist-high elephant grass, too exhausted to talk, some of them falling asleep immediately.

"Damn good to see you boys!" said the captain between breaths, shaking hands and slapping rumps all around. "Thought we'd lost ya for sure. Did ya take any wounded or KIA?"

"None," replied Mars.

"We lost three," said Foley. "We stripped their gear and buried 'em best we could with their dog tags. Hated to do that but we'd no choice. Silva, Skeet, and the Hardluck Kid."

"The Kid," said Pinball, turning away his face. "Well, he was one of 'em never meant to get outa this war alive."

"This is a bad place, Captain," said Waldo. "We've got no cover in the open like this."

"I know it. But it was the only landmark I could spot

quick. I figure right now the thing to do is to get into those trees on the south side, circle up, and sack out. Conservin' energy's more important than anything else—we're all bushed. Then, before dawn, we move due south and keep movin' until we're in easy range of the downed chopper before we cut southeast to search for that MIA."

"Good plan. But we got some units on our tail."

"You said fifty in the unit you were followin'?"

"Fifty plus."

"Fifty less," said the Bee, "after all that steel."

"We ambushed a unit of about twenty," said Foley. "We didn't wanta do it, but we had no choice. They acted like they wanted to slow us down for another element to clobber us."

"That's right," said Sar'n Mars. "Those fifty were comin' after you."

"So we can figure on forty to fifty leftovers, then," said Waldo. "What've we got—thirty-one effectives?"

"We gotta find that guy from the chopper and bug out, fast," said the Bee.

"If we had to fight Chuck, we could dig in," said Pinball. "Chuck'd need four to five times our number to push us out of a good position. We could dig in and call for help."

"We've got nothin' to call with, Pinball," said Foley. "Waldo, how's your radio?"

"Finished. Battery's dead."

"Well, at least you got that fire in. We got good batts but no radios that'll broadcast more'n a klick. Find Kansas City and get his spare batt. Now, we've been here too long. Bee, Pin, Knobs, spread the word—south—now. Sar'n Mars, stay with me. Let's move out.

Well before false dawn the two Chuck captains rousted their frightened and red-eyed soldiers and led them cautiously into the forest area devastated by the eight-inch. It was as though the hand of some hot-blooded round-eye god had crushed down through the jungle canopy, scooped up earth and trees and men, and let it all dribble in ruins between his fingers, leaving heaps of black seeping mud and pits filled with slime and jutting bone.

There had been no wounded straggling in last night. Nor had there been any cats to stop them—the eight-inch had driven the big cats into their holes. No, the wounded— three of them—had found each other and huddled together against a shattered tree trunk and, together, had bled to death, too much in shock from the bombardment to realize what was happening to them.

False dawn seemed to come up out of the particles of earth. They knew Yank choppers would be there soon to gloat over this victory as they had two days ago when more sudden hellfire had smashed half of Captain Dong's company. They stripped the three dead of material and ID, threw them into a crater, and buried them. They collected the pieces of the other nine KIA and did the same with them.

Then they tramped downtrail to the site of Bravo's ambush to see what had become of the already broken twenty-man company that had been following Bravo. They found ten of them shot to pieces and four more whimpering in the trees. As for the remaining six, they had simply disappeared. They would eventually show up at HQ telling lies of heroism. The two captains had the bodies buried and found the common grave of Silva, Skeet, and the Hardluck Kid—stripped, with only one dog tag each—and recovered them. So these weren't Nungs! They were Americans after all! What had gotten into them? Why weren't they acting like GIs? They got the story of Bravo's guerilla ambush of the twenty-man company from the four whimpering survivors, and liked hearing none of it. With the full flush of dawn, they heard the clattering of three choppers over-head—Raiby's photo mission as ordered by Colonel Yoden—and barreled south into the deeper woods to await whatever fresh disaster their own valley had in mind for them. They were beaten enough to radio the truth to higher, and to beg for help.

The grunt Batco, Peter Yoden, had not slept for his rage. At 0700 he stormed into DeeTOC red-eyed and angry, furious for two hours until the air-recon photos—eight-by-ten black-and-white glossies—were presented to him. "Ah, ha!" he sneered. "Show these to that insolent redleg FDO. Sergeant Raiby, get over here! Look at these. Eight-inch can turn over a good two acres of jungle, all right, but there's not a gook eyeball in any of it. Ha!"

"Pardon, Colonel," said the bespectacled photo analyst who had brought the pics. He tugged a photo from the clump in Yoden's hand and laid it on top. It was the view from a higher altitude showing the target zone and the surrounding canopy. In the thick upper branches of a tree, where an eight-inch round had thrown it, was a man's leg dressed in khaki pantleg and truck-tire Chuck sandal.

"Oh, no," groaned Yoden. It was no longer a bad joke or Raiby's aberration. It was real, whatever that meant in Vietnam. "We got somebody down there in the valley all by himself, and no way to get him out!" cried Yoden. He shouted for his maps and his G-2 intel officer and they went to work piecing together the evidence of the last seventy-two hours, a triumphant Raiby as narrator.

And there it was, plain as day on all the maps, on all the back azimuths, on the radio intercepts, on the redhaze—someone was moving south away from Baldy and the first day's battle that had claimed the life of Bravo Company. He was being followed, without doubt, by at least two company-size elements of VC/NVA. He had called fire on them twice and he had somehow attacked once, perhaps twice, a unit he had found in his path—but attacked with what? How? He had single-handedly chopped them to bits and he had kept humping south. The evidence was right there to see. "But, good Christ," said Yoden, clutching the charts, "how can he do all this? Listen, if he's an officer he deserves a Silver Star for this. If he's enlisted, I swear I'll see he gets the BS with all the Valor-Vs and oakleaf clusters I can cram on it." He peered at the map. "He's doing great outstanding work. He's single-handedly drawing away from Baldy forces that could be causing the paratroopers extra grief, and they've plenty of that already. It's taken them three days to gain 150 meters and that ain't halfway up the mountain yet." He stared fiercely at the map. "But I don't understand it—how could one guy do all that?"

"May not be just one, sir," said the G-2 captain. "Remember, there were two bods missing from Bravo—the FO and that buck sergeant, George Bee."

"That's right! It's two guys then. But, even two guys?"

"Can't be more than that, sir," said the G-2. "Two can evade the sniffers, redhaze, photo recons. Any more than that, we'd have seen it right here." He tapped the charts and photos.

The landline clattered and Raiby answered. When he put down the handset, he reported, "Colonel, choppers just back from Baldy to refuel and rearm say they spotted a company-size element moving into heavy canopy two klicks south of Baldy."

"Moving up on the paras, you mean?"

"No, sir. Moving south."

"South, Raiby? They *can't* be movin' south. They *wouldn't* be movin' south. The fight's up on the mountain."

"South, they said, sir."

"Did those choppers take them under fire?"

"They were outa ammo."

"Raiby, nobody sends two companies plus after two lost GIs. Nobody then sends a third company after two guys when they've got a hell of a fight going for them on Baldy."

"Yes, sir, I know," said Raiby. "They would do it if it was more than just two guys, though, sir."

"Now, Sarge," cut in Second Lieutenant Edgar Engle, usually closed-mouth in the presence of his burly, red-eyed, and frightening Batco, "let's not worry the colonel with your crazy theories."

"Shut up, kid," said Yoden. "What's your crazy theory, Raiby?"

"It's Bravo, sir."

"Who?"

"Bravo's down there. They're after Bravo."

"It would make sense, sir," said the G-2 bravely. "They'd send three companies after one. That's the way you fight in the jungle—overwhelming superiority or nothing."

"But Bravo Company of what battalion?" asked the mystified Yoden.

"Of this battalion, sir," said Raiby.

"What?" shouted Yoden. "You two are nuts! Bravo was nuked away. I saw the bods myself."

"It's Bravo's FO who's calling fire, sir," said Raiby.

"And it's on our battalion freak that our radio intercepts have been picking up some strange trans using the Bravo call sign," added the G-2.

"We got us two lost boys down there," said Colonel Yoden. "They've fallen in with a unit from an AO to our south that has gotten off its track and into our territory and they are fighting their way south to their support base. That's the answer. In fact, looking at this map you can see that if they continue their line of march for two to three days more, they'll be in Phu Bon Area of Ops. Waldo and the Bee've fallen in with some Phu Bon Mike Force, that's all. Engle, get on the horn to PB and give me a sitrep asap." He scowled at Raiby before he put a fatherly hand on the sergeant's shoulder and said gently, "Bravo, my foot, Sergeant. When's your R and R due?"

"Six weeks, sir."

"Going to see your old lady in Hawaii, I hope? Good. Put in your papers this week, Sergeant. You're going on holiday asap. You need it, buddy." The colonel turned his sympathetic face at his G-2; the sympathy faded to a glower. "You, Willy, keep outa my sight for a couple days. It'll take me that long to forget my G-2 believes in ghosts. Engle, you're the only one around here with any sense. I won't forget that on your efficiency report." He glowered around at his staff officers cowering away from him, shook his head in disbelief, and stomped out of the bunker.

It had not been an easy decision for the 95-Bravo VC regimental commander to make to send a third company south after those mysterious American guerilla units. Despite the hysteria of the two field commanders—Captains Dong and Nguyen, men he had always trusted for coolheadedness—there was no disputing the damage these small units had managed to achieve. If all reports were to be believed (and who could really believe field reports from grunts?), the Americans, operating in three tiny independent commands until they had linked up last night, had accounted for forty killed, wounded or missing. That was incredible when on Old Baldy (the 95 Bravos called it that, too) five typically understrength Yank paratroop battalions with gunnies, zoomies, spookies, and plenty of arty had, in three days' battle, cost the 95-B (hastily dug in after Bravo Company had transitted the mountain in pursuit of the downed chopper in order to seal Bravo in the valley) only fifteen casualties. Against that the 95-Bravos with a boost from the NVA Yellow Division (though they were mostly poorly trained and inexperienced clerks) had wiped out the forty-two men of Bravo Company and (according to radio intercepts and medevac calls) cost the paratroops another six KIA and seventeen WIA. It had been a very profitable seventy-two hours for Uncle Ho.

Unfortunately, these victories were all the 95-B could hope for—there were just too many Yanks to make a clean, field-clearing triumph. That was the way it always was, for both sides. It was the basis for the occasionally interrupted peace of the five armies of the highlands. Still, the commander could have sent the third company sweeping into the paratroops' rear to rack up a better body count. He had sighed when he thought of the glory of claiming the elimination of, say, another whole company of Yanks, of paratroopers at that. But he had done the prudent thing, and the prudent thing was what he always had to do as he was always outmanned and outgunned—he had sent the third company south after this mystery guerilla unit. Now, before another twenty-four hours had passed, he would pull everyone off Old Baldy and leave the barren mountain for the surprise and amusement of the paratroops. He could imagine the chagrin of their battalion commanders when they found their VC enemy suddenly vanished into the forest. How would they write their reports to their higher to win the glory they wanted? he wondered. The commander laughed. No, killing Bravo Company would be enough for him. It was time to withdraw and to write his own reports.

Bravo Company had made a similar decision and used similar tactics to get away from the combined units of the two Chuck captains following. Bravo divided itself into three parts, exfiltrating the woods in which it had lain the remainder of the night, and then rejoined its parts a thousand meters farther south. Waldo's was the only radio that could reach base camp or the somewhat closer LZ Action so they used a fresh battery on it. Though they kept radio silence to avoid Chuck's triangulating on them, Waldo called in periodic laagers and sitreps to assure that no errant air-cav choppers mistook Bravo for Chuck. Most of Waldo's commo was with his own FDC, who accepted that someone who could shoot well was using a dead man's call sign; FDC was not interested in questioning further. But for fire support coordination and to keep the gunnies off his back, Waldo had to go up to the blueleg net to call Raiby in DeeTOC.

"Is that really you, two-four, over," Raiby's voice cried in Waldo's ear.

"Of course, it's me. Ya got my coordinates in shackle or not, over."

"Roger, I say 'em back"—Raiby repeated the coded laager—"But, two-four, who's with you—Pagan-four? Over."

"Roger, Pagan-four is here, over."

"*All* of four, over?"

"That's a rog, except the wounded you evacked three days ago." said Waldo, growing impatient. "This is our plan. From this laager we're headin' azimuth one–eight–five–zero to vicinity new target area I gave you in shackle. Got that, over."

"One–eight–five–zero to target. What's target, over."

"What the hell were we sent down here to find, over," said Waldo in irritation.

"Right on, two-four," exclaimed Raiby. "You mean the chopper? Over."

"Rog. Ya got new intel on it for us? We figure there's a guy still down there, over."

Raiby's voice was silent. (In his fluorescent bunker he was wondering what to say—the chopper had crashed four days ago and three days ago Bravo Company had, as far as the army was concerned, ceased to exist. The bones and ash of the three dead that Bravo had recovered were en route to Burgerland for burial. Now Raiby was talking to one of the two missing from Bravo, who claimed he had Bravo—call sign Pagan-four—with him, and that they were going after the chopper again.) Raiby's voice said: "Negative, negative new info, over."

"Rog. Next commo will be when we strike our new laager, out."

Raiby in his bunker stared at the radio on which a man with a dead unit had just signed off. Engle and the G-2 captain stared at Raiby. "Strange what a little static can make you believe, right, Cap?" said Engle.

"Yeah, weird." The G-2 glanced at Engle's hand still on the landline. "You talk to Phu Bon AO?"

"Just finished," said Engle.

"What did they say?" asked Raiby.

"No Phu Bon units, Mike or other, in our valley." Engle gritted his teeth. "They've also been following the trans of whoever that is down in the valley. Get them lima-charlie, in fact, no static. Trouble is, PB is an Arvin AO so all their RTOs are Viets and speak no English. They can hear but they don't understand."

"There goes the colonel's theory that Waldo and the Bee fell in with some wandering Mikes," said Raiby.

"It was a good theory," said the G-2. "What do we give him for a replacement—that Bravo has risen from its body bags and is down there taking revenge on Chuck? Damn, there's gotta be a logical explanation. I'm authorizing a sniffer to sweep those coordinates this 'two-four' gave us. If there's a unit down there, we'll smell 'em, count heads, and make eyeball-to-eyeball contact. Engle, you check with the Fourth Division AO to our west and see if maybe their air cav inserted some Beanies on the wrong side of the border? Do it. Now, until we've got a good explanation for the colonel, we don't let our imaginations run away with us, right, Raiby? Good." The bookish intelligence officer adjusted his glasses firmly to emphasize his order and went out.

Bravo, in its three pieces, moved south. Captain Foley took the center column, the Second Platoon led by black, bowlegged Sergeant Louis Knobs with Fruitcake loping along on point, and Enrique B-2 Saavedra, his eyes sunk deeper in bruised sacks of worry, as the captain's bodyguard. Little Corporal Myron Pinball Bagirov, with the shotgun he feared and hated, would do Foley's map reading for him. They took with them the six walking wounded and Kansas City's radio. There were only three working radios in the company.

On the eastern flank tramped Waldo with Georgie Bee and First Plat. On the western flank Sar'n Mars, curling his drooping mustache in his fingers, led the Mortar Platoon augmented with Deerslayer and his big knife.

They were reasonably apportioned and reasonably well armed but low on ammo and food. Water they could always find. Some of them had augmented their poor supplies with what they could hastily steal from the bods of the dead Chucks—they had with them three Ak47 assault rifles, a prize souvenir Chicom pistol, and an NVA bayonet. Ammo for those enemy weapons was low, too: Chuck had carried no more than twenty rounds for each rifle and only two magazines for the pistol. He, too, fought a cut-rate war. They tramped south yearning to fall upon a richly equipped NVA platoon to kill and rob. They dreamed no more of the war's end.

After four hours they had marched five hundred meters, a tremendous accomplishment under steaming triple-canopy where they had chosen not to use machetes but to keep secure silence. Foley leading the middle element called a halt for zonk and grub. Second Plat fell out like marionettes released from their strings, half of them passing out where they fell. They were exhausted and they had fought a running battle with Chuck. Foley gave permission for some quick fires made of C-4 explosive putty in hand-dug pits.

Although Dong and Nguyen had lighter jungle through which to lead their combined unit, the morning had been a grim one for them, too. They had barely finished their burial chores, cowered away from the heli photo recon mission Raiby had sent out, and crossed the site of the company Bravo had destroyed (collecting the four whimpering leftovers), when a soldier spotted in the mud the prize they all wanted—a souvenir M16 with a cracked stock—and thoughtlessly pick it up. Of course the Yanks had booby-trapped it with a grenade. The man was killed and two more wounded. They performed another hasty burial and hurried on, wondering how Bravo had had the time and presence of mind in its flight to set that trap. They marched into the first pungi, a sharpened stake stabbed butt-first into the earth, the point disguised by brush and just waist high. The first victim died miserably, his body spilling around him as he shrieked like a tortured cat.

Now wary and nearing demoralization, they picked their way through the forest realizing that Bravo had had the stakes prepared long in advance and that its rearguard had simply stabbed them into the ground as they ran in case Bravo was followed in their night bugout. Grim. Mean. Terrifying.

Meantime, higher was shrieking at them insisting that they pursue the enemy with more dispatch. They shied away from the trail Bravo had left and, keeping one flank in contact with it, moved west. They were surprised to find the morning sun well up over the valley at the moment they plunged from the forest edge and peered across into the empty grass field where Bravo had reassembled itself. The radio crackled. Dong answered it expecting to hear more of higher's abuse but he got the news instead that two more radio intercept posts had caught enough of the Raiby-Waldo trans to triangulate a fair fix. He was astonished and frightened how close the enemy was—within eyesight, if the enemy had not marched on. Higher had only two commands to accompany this news—watch for the third company coming down to help and move due south now to either strike in the flank and hold Bravo for the third company or to get ahead of the enemy and shove him against the third company. Quite reasonable orders, the two captains agreed, if this were a reasonable enemy unit they were following. They assigned three men to accompany the wounded back to base, leaving them only thirty-nine effectives; they reapportioned weapons and ammo; then they led out south, a fresh grimness coming into them all: they had to destroy Bravo Company or Bravo, through some perverseness of the natural order that had once granted the valley to Chuck, would surely destroy them.

LZ Action lay at the foot of the grim white bluffs of the Mang Yang Pass beyond which—through the wind-cut gorge 150 meters deep where Highway 19 had been laid—were the 1,000 graves of the dead Frenchmen of Mobile Group 100 who had fought and lost a great battle here just before the final French defeat at Dien Bien Phu. Action was a fire base, home to six 105mm howitzers of Action Battery of Waldo's battalion, the guns laid out in the modified standard format of staggered guns presenting a slightly smaller battery front than the field manuals demanded. But the modified front allowed the tubes to be swiveled 360 degrees to fire in any direction and to pump beehive rounds—cannisters of thousands of tiny steel arrows—at any enemy close enough to warrant. Half of the fire base was dug into the hard, bright earth, with rifle slits at ground level. Its distinguishing feature—as was the feature of all fire bases in that Area of Ops (because a previous arty Batco had been a frustrated engineer)—was the thirty-foot steel, concrete, and sandbag tower erected by the gunbunnies. The bunnies had hung on the tower their battleflags—California Republic, Dixie, Don't Tread On Me, Spirit of '76, and an assortment of colored bras and panties won in battles in Sin City. But for the battalion commanders, grunt and redleg alike, the tower was not only a lookout but a grand place from which to play General Patton, peering deep into both the Mang Yang through which the convoys sped and into the valley.

They were there now: the infantry Batco, burly Colonel Yoden with his gray hair; the artillery Batco, a lieutenant colonel, Texas John S. Aylward; and Brigadier General

William "Mountain" King of the paratroop brigade slogging its way up Old Baldy and commanding general of this Area of Operations. (He was called "Mountain" because, when frustrated in battle, he would spread napalm and burn mountains to kill Chucks; his own troops called him "Mad Mountain.") They were now watching the fight on Baldy—like a silent movie: lots of flash but no bang at that distance. "Can't believe it," said the general, tapping his manicured nails on his big brass belt buckle with the huge general's star. "We've been on that mountain four days and we've got only sixty-five confirmed kills. Now you tell me"—he glowered at Colonel Yoden—"that your intel says Chuck is pulling *off* the mountain? Incredible! We haven't hurt him that bad yet." He put a cigarette into his mouth, chewing on the filter as an aide flicked a lighter. "I don't want to leave the mountain until we've got two hundred confirmed KIA. I didn't bring five batts down here to walk away without a lot—a *lot*—of kills." He glowered at the Batco. "This op was your idea, Colonal. It's turning into a fiasco. Find a way to stop the seepage of Chucks off my mountain. Find me some kills, asap."

"Yes, General." Yoden turned ashen-faced to the paratroop captains there assembled—ragged, dirty, the general had brought these company commanders from the field into LZ Action for one of his patented pep talks—and was astounded to find that of the fourteen company commanders sent onto the mountain, only nine survived. In the five half-strength battalions that composed most of Mountain King's brigade—less than a thousand combat soldiers—the general had taken fifty KIA and double that WIA. Fiasco was not the right word for it; disaster was. Without some very creative report writing, or a good VC body count, the general was going to get slapped down by his higher command for this episode, and that meant Yoden was going to lose his command right here. No Legion of Honor. No exit in a blaze of glory. No, in little more than a week Yoden would go home to the hoots of the newspaper-men wanting to know why he—the Batco, not the general—had wasted American lives on Old Baldy, wasted them in a losing war.

That was not the half of it for Peter Yoden. Back in Burgerland he had a wife, fat and graying, and a child, a daughter. Every time he looked at her, he regretted that she had taken so much from his side of the family: She was taller than he, over six feet, big-boned enough to be a pro linebacker, and there just weren't that many men her size to marry her. So Yoden had shoved her into college to get her a profession so she could take care of herself in life. In his neighborhood where everybody knew Yoden as "Peter" and not "Colonel," there were other people—young ones, mostly, his daughter's college friends—who hated Yoden for being part of this war and who scorned his undateable, giant daughter for the father's sake. Yoden would rather have killed college students than Chucks to spare his daughter her torment, but now he was 10,000 miles from home and helpless, and he knew that even were he back home he would be helpless. In ten days he would be home and he would be helpless. Why hadn't he been smart and politicked for a European assignment staring down the Russkies, and taken his wife and daughter to Germany? And then slide into an early retirement? No, he had been too smart to be smart. He had wanted that general's star on his shoulder. The only way to get that star was to prove himself in war. There was only one war around. He had had to join it. It was the worst mistake of his life, and there would be no star for compensation, and perhaps no daugh-ter, either. Shame could drive her from him.

"Sir," said one of the dirty paratroop captains, startling Yoden from his grim reverie, "we've a good idea where the Chucks are drawing off to and suggest we do the same."

"What's that?" demanded the general, chewing the filter of his cig. Though King was a nicotine addict, he smoked filtered cigarettes. He was not afraid of bullets—in these modern times, generals don't die in combat—but he was terrified of cancer, a more indiscriminate killer.

"For three to four days we've all been intercepting trans from another U.S. unit south of us in the valley."

"What?" goggled Yoden.

"Sure. Must be a unit coming up from Phu Bon A0. They're kickin' tail down there, sure as hell. We think"— the captain motioned to the other captains—"that Chuck is drawing off forces from Baldy, from a fight he can't win, to move south to annihilate this other unit."

"Leapfrog," said the general.

"Right, General. He wants a little victory if he can't have a big one."

"What?" demanded Yoden again.

"We let this southern unit draw Chuck off the mountain, Colonel Yoden," explained the general in his arrogant voice. "Let them be the lure. Then we use my choppers to extract my troops from Baldy and drop them on Chuck when his back is turned." The general chomped on his filter. "We soften the target area with gunnies and zoomies and I go home with a victory instead of a disaster."

"But there *is* no unit down south, General," blurted Yoden.

"Of course there is."

"We checked it. PB has no one that far north. It's all just freak static. There may be one FO and one grunt lost down there from Bravo Company, if the cats didn't get them, but that's it."

General King glared at his dirty captains. "What've you got to say?"

"We stick with it, General. Whoever's down there, Chuck is exfiltrating the mountain—we've seen high-speed trails he's cut moving south. That unit is drawing him off the mountain."

"If Chuck believes, I believe it, Colonel," said King to

Yoden. The general glanced at the horizon. "We've got six more hours daylight. Colonel, get the choppers and tracks ready for extraction of my troops asap. Ten secs after my boys are out, I want that mountain nuked. Tell the zoomies to spread napalm all over it. We fly my boys into your base camp, Colonel," he said, calculation in his eye, "until we've got confirmation of all this activity in the valley. If it merits, we'll dump my boys on Chuck and eat him alive."

And if not, thought Yoden, your troops will be safe in base camp ready to fly home the same day, leaving me here with the peace of the five armies destroyed, the blood of your fifty dead and of Bravo Company on my hands, my efficiency report wrecked, and my career—what will be left of that? When the newspapers get hold of this, what will her classmates say to my daughter about her father? What will she say to me?

The 95-Bravo VC regimental commander in his tile-walled, electric-lit underground bunker was delighted to have an opponent of the caliber of Brigadier General "Mad Mountain" King. King had come to Vietnam from a different era of war; his version of surprise and maneuver by helicopter gave ample noisy warning to his enemies, enemies who never fought him without the advantage he gave them. The commander watched Old Baldy burn with napalm in the clear evening, wondering how he was going to make this disaster look good in his reports to higher: Baldy had represented his safest infiltration route from which to attack road convoys; built into Baldy over generations of war was an excellent tunnel system, now crushed by Phantoms' bombs and napalm, where the 95-B and the NVA Yellow Division had an advance HQ and a field hospital prepared, sealed up and ready for use. It was now lost. Worse, despite the unspoken peace of the five armies he now had five battalions of Yank paras flitting over the valley in helis, something that had never happened before, and, he prayed, would never happen again. At least he had extracted his men before the napalm fire came in; the choppers had given him plenty of warning for that. It was not beyond reason that in the near future the 95-B could go back up on Baldy and open up that field hospital and advance HQ—the paras had not found them because the Phantoms had buried the sealed entrances.

But General King, like all his go-go type, would be easy to beat: just give him nothing to fight. Bore him a few days, a week at most. Hope he did not get lucky and stumble over another field hospital dug into another mountain or an arms cache. He woud grow tired of inaction and go someplace else looking for easier pickings. The higher they got in the American army, the easier a Yank officer wanted his war. So the commander passed the order—disappear!—and the units he had brought down off Baldy seeped into the jungle, into spider holes, caves, tunnels, and were gone.

The commander then prepared his reports in leisure. Radio intercepts told him General King had 50 KIA and perhaps three times that number WIA, plus those who had stumbled and fallen getting off the mountain, so the commander reported a healthier 112 KIA and 250 estimated WIA to higher. How, he thought, to describe the action down south? What could be said about one small Yank outfit that prowled the valley like Red Indians and had destroyed or tied down three VC companies? There was nothing to be said about that that would show credit on the commander. It was best left out of the report until it could be resolved.

Foley's voice on the radio said, "All elements, swing southeast on azimuth one–seven hundred. Look to link up at the flanks. We're gettin' close. We'll sweep to the chopper before nightfall and laager there if we must, over."

"Roger, out," said Mars.

"Rog, out," said Waldo. "Let's go, Bee. One–seven hundred toward the chopper and tell the right flank guards to watch for Daddy."

"We gonna make that whole thousand meters tonight? That's a hell of a march."

"We gotta. Let's move."

They tramped through the forest that was growing blacker as tropic night swept over that corner of Asia. They tramped quickly. Like the moment four days before when they had broken from dreamless deathly sleep on Old Baldy to charge downslope into the fight to save the minesweep tank, they moved with hot determination, careless of fatigue and hunger, with professionalism. They believed themselves unconquerable in pursuit of their mission: This time they would succeed.

All three Bravo elements crashed together into the clearing at the base of a small hill, the clearing burned by the falling chopper. Pages of aircraft handbooks showered down on them from the treetops. Sections of light metal that were strewn across the jungle canopy slid and crashed to earth as they chopped through the brush to find the chopper as Waldo had found it before—only the tail boom and its one little rotor whole, the rotor cranking over in the light breeze, all the rest burned to ash.

Captain Foley, rubbing sweat from his forehead with a black-gloved hand, shouted, "Chuck must know we're here. Circle the area. Set out claymores and pungi stakes. Machine-gunners, choose your fields of fire. Waldo, get us some D-Ts plotted. Sar'n Mars," Foley said, "get out there and find that last crewman. He's out there alive, I know he is. We didn't hike a million miles for another pocketful of bones."

"Hey, hey!" cried a startled voice in the trees north of the clearing.

Suddenly five GIs stampeded into the clearing dragging a big man in a ragged flight suit, blood all over his face and chest, and the man was shouting, "I'm alive! I'm alive!"

Foley stood a moment, dumbfounded, one hand on his glasses, staring at the airman. Then he and Bravo Company swarmed around the man, slapping his back, demanding his name, raising a cheer. Weldon Cobb, the medic, jammed himself through the crowd to use his last material to clean the airman's metal-slashed face and to bandage his broken wrists. They gave him water, bourbon, and chocolate. Mars's warning voice said over the triumphant hubbub: "We better move out, Captain. Been here too long."

"Right. Rog," replied Foley, grinning like a fool, savoring this rare victory. "How many grenades we got, Sar'n?"

"Niner."

"Bee, take two of em and booby-trap the wreck. All you who were cuttin' pungi, mount 'em and then saddle up quick. Waldo, plot fire on this laager but tell FDC not to shoot it until you say so. You'll call fire when you hear the booby traps blow."

"Saddle up!" said Mars. "Company column. Fruitcake, take the lead. Captain, which way?"

"Due east. I wanta get into the mountains and climb outa this filthy valley just as quick as we can."

"Move out, Fruity. Flank guards! Pinball, your squad has the rear. Let's go!"

Bravo Company slipped into the forest, moving with speed and care, their fatigue and hunger gone in the flush of their triumph: They had saved the survivor! They had *known* he was still there, and, like good soldiers, they had not abandoned him.

11

WALDO, SWITCHING FROM redleg to blueleg nets as he plunged through the jungle, reported the good news to Raiby for him to pass the word higher.

In DeeTOC, Lieutenant Engle gaped at the radio in fright. "That can't be! They're all dead!"

Raiby cheered across the bunker: "It's Bravo Company! They're climbin' outa the valley and they've got a survivor from the downed chopper!"

The G-2 captain whooped, throwing his army baseball cap into the air.

The landline jangled. Engle answered. "It's battalion FDC. They've got a firemission from two-four and want to know if it's safe to fire," he whispered to Raiby out of paled lips.

"There's not another soul down there but Bravo," said Raiby. "Tell 'em to fire."

The blueleg radio crackled with the voice of the Batco: "You got contact down there?" said Colonel Yoden without preliminaries or call signs. "I want to know what the hell's going on—that unit is supposed to be in the morgue, over."

"We already got a sniffer on the way down there, over," replied the G-2 officer.

"Good. Out."

The G-2 captain shouted across the bunker to a lieuten-ant: "Get a sniffer over Bravo's laager asap or Yoden will have our butts."

At LZ Action cheers rose from the gunbunnies clustered around the stepdown entrance to the battery FDC bunker. In the tower, Brigadier General King stared narrowly at Yoden and the artillery Lieutenant Colonel Texas John Aylward. "What do you two mean you've checked it out? You *can't* have checked it out. There *is* a unit down south and if it's not from Phu Bon then it's from Fourth Div or from somewhere else."

"General, it's not PB or the Fourth, we know that," said Yoden.

"Then who the hell is it?"

The two battalion commanders glanced at each other and gazed together out the open window toward napalm-burn-ing Old Baldy where dozens of slicks were lifting off the paratroopers to return them to base camp. This was a cautious general when the fighting went against him—he would put those troopers in base, burn the mountain, and claim a limited victory. If, in a day or so, they—meaning the local battalion commanders, Yoden and Aylward— could not produce another target for King's airborne, King would take them home to his base in the north, and blame the local commanders for wasting the energies of five batts of paras plus a big piece of the Department of Procure-ment's war budget. Vietnam was not going to end happily for the two battalion commanders. "Well, General," said Yoden at last as Aylward turned to stare at the Batco, wondering how Yoden was going to get them both out of this mess, "we may not know precisely what unit that is down there—"

"I'm relieved to hear you're not saying it's Bravo Com-pany."

"—but that unit is doing us a service. Without doubt it's

attracting Chucks. It may even be attracting the 95-Bravo elements pulled off Baldy. I'd suggest we send some of your airborne"—he motioned toward the choppers lifting off the mountain—"down there to meet and greet this unit when it comes up out of the valley."

The general put another cig between his lips, grinding the filter in his teeth, as his starched-fatigue aide jumped to light it. "We know where they're coming out?"

"We can pick a spot and tell them to expect us there."

"They'll want to be extracted," said the general. "They'll want some medals for this." He gazed at the two advancement-hungry, worried colonels staring at him. "If we don't pull a good body count on this mish, issuing medals wholesale and writing up this unit's action as our own might just get us all out of the fire."

"That's what I was thinking, General," said Yoden, trying to keep the desperation from his voice.

King was being cautious; he was on the verge of winning a paper victory—a very small victory with too many American casualties called Operation Old Baldy. Or he could throw it all over for one chance with a lost unit that had blundered into a nest of Chucks and make out of that a real fight and a real victory. "We'd sure surprise hell outa Chuckie if we were to divert two companies from Baldy and drop them in the south to meet this unit at first light tomorrow, wouldn't we?"

He's talking himself into it, thought Yoden. "That we would, General," he said with bright optimism.

"All right, boys. Show me your intel—redhaze number one—from the past couple hours. Let's get good commo with this unit. Let's see *if* this is really such a smart idea. We got fifteen minutes to decide, no more. If it's go, we divert the next two companies off Baldy, and they've gotta spend one damn scary night in Chuck's valley all alone."

The answer was "Go." This operation had started with the sacrifice and annihilation of Bravo Company, gotten too

194

big with the entrance of the paratroops and gotten out of hand with a wasteful, victoryless battle on Old Baldy. No one could afford to let it end with the annihilation of another American unit, unknown and unnamed though it was.

"We're gonna get outa here!" Kansas City whispered nervously to Captain Foley as they tramped together through the darkening forest. "Higher is sendin' two companies to meet us at these coords"—hands trembling, he gave the captain his notepad—"at first light—and they're bringin' slicks to get us out!"

Foley, puzzling with the coordinates on his map in the fading evening light, was relieved when Kansas tapped his finger on the right place—the eastern side of the mountain range they had begun to climb. He cursed softly, uncharacteristic of the Missouri village parson he used to be: They had one more unavoidable night in the valley—no choppers could be expected to come in after dark—and one more mountain range to slog over.

But this time there was someone waiting for them on the far side—two companies of paras. It was true: They were going to make it! "Pass the word," said Foley, folding his map into his front thigh pocket and pushing on uphill.

They had crossed the small foothills into which the chopper had crashed and moved seventy-five meters up the western slope of the mountain range, full darkness all about them and the time on them to slink into the forest to set up their protective circle, when two quick *thuds* came to them thinly through the jungle—the Bee's booby traps on the wrecked heli. "Chuck's right behind us!" groaned Kansas, jumping around.

Mars came out of the darkness next to Foley. "We've made only a couple hundred meters max, Captain. The men are bushed and Chuck is too close."

"Rog. This is trail's end for Chuck, Sar'n. Pass the word,

Kansas—halt. Take five but everyone cuts three pungi, minimum. We'll stake this end of the trail, Sar'n Mars, then we'll cut due south a couple hundred and circle up. Where's Waldo?"

"Here, Captain."

"Chuck is on the wreck. Call your fire now."

"Rog." Waldo stepped away, clapping his handset to ear and mouth.

Overhead, they heard the wild scurrying clatter of the G-2 captain's sniffership as it ran back to base, its pilots terrified at their close call—they'd turned up the thirty-nine VC/NVA of the combined units, strangely marked by two grenade flashes, and the third company moving south along the ridgeline. The sniffer dived over the mountain ridge into the protection of the two paratroop companies circled-up and dug-in in usual style, their perimeter heavy with MGs and claymores. Then the sniffer raced past Baldy under the arcing fire of the eight-inch howitzer shells streaking down on the chopper wreck and the combined units.

Bravo Company, its pungi trap set, plunged south into the black jungle.

It was not the combined units of the two Chuck captains that fell into Bravo's nasty trap on the trail; it was the third company from the NVA Yellow Division, led by Lieutenant Giap, a company of the best available men from the Division's rear elements—battle-trained cooks and clerks. Moving at great speed on ridgetop high-speed trails, depending on the combined units ahead to keep it appraised of trouble, the third company drove its lead elements onto the pungi stakes, the men screaming and writhing as they died, awakening the big cats to howl in their lairs at the moment a great shattering, earth-turning disaster was brought down on the combined units at the chopper by Waldo's artillery fire. Out-flung metal clattered around the NVA company; the once-clear evening air was dense with bitter cordite and dust. Lieutenant Giap turned from the shriekings of his own dying to see the uphill scrabble of the bloody remnant of the two combined units and himself broke combat silence to shout in his Northern accent his warning about the pungi.

Of the thirty-nine effectives in the combined units, twelve—covered with other men's blood and brains, dripping with mud—staggered choking and white-eyed from the black jungle to collapse at the feet of the startled NVA clerks. Captain Dong was among the survivors, the only officer or NCO left alive, tears streaming down his melted face as he thought how close he had come to never again wallowing on his soft, fat wife. The NVA lieutenant gazed at the 95-Bravos and thought, These are the much-scorned guerilla-fighters, the men the great Tet battles had destroyed, the men the NVA sacrificed in order to clear them from the political wars to allow more tractable units, more political units, more conventional units of Northerners to have the glory of the great final push against the Yanks to win the war. But he knew these were also the great warriors, and if there was a Yank outfit down there in the valley's night that could destroy three VC companies in four days of running battle, then his motley collection of overage, overweight clerks and cooks had no chance at all.

Lieutenant Giap peered into the suddenly frightening jungle night and ordered his men to slip offtrail and set up a defensive ring in the trees, Nung-style. Then, despite the shame of it, he called the Chuck regimental commander for help.

The 95-Bravo commander received Giap's radio call in the middle of a flurry of surprising and discouraging reports: Not all of the paras had been withdrawn to base camp, it seemed. Two companies had been shuttled south. In the typical noisy confusion of the Yank evacuation of Old Baldy, no one had noticed—or no one had reported— that some choppers flown east toward the Yankee base camp had ducked behind a mountain range to flit south, to insert two companies dangerously close to the units the commander had directed south to deal with the Yank guerilla element. He stared at the decoded message in his hand and wanted to laugh. It was the first time he had seen the Yanks use their own noisy confusion to hide a surprise move. "Mad Mountain" King was going to leave this war with a better education than he had brought into it.

Now, on top of that shock, the commander received Lieutenant Giap's report that the two combined units tracking the Yank guerillas had been blown away by more of that hideous artillery fire, and Giap's NVA company—old men who had seen battle too long ago to remember much of it— was capable of little more than annoying the Yanks. The commander had counted on the NVA only for bods and bullets; he had expected his own combined units to mastermind and to lead the annihilation of the Yanks. Now he was stuck with a major battle in the morning and he was unprepared. He could lose the NVA company, too, and he could not afford to lose it—liaison was already poor with the Yellow Division, and his 95-Bravos needed the Yellow's supply dumps and underground hospitals. Further, he had not done so well on Baldy that he could justify in his reports losing another company—he had already lost three in the valley! He began to sweat with anxiety. He cursed himself, the Yanks, the war, Uncle Ho. Three companies utterly destroyed and by what—forty Yanks at most? He wanted to scream. His highers *would* be screaming. He cursed himself for being so stupid as to underestimate a Yank guerilla unit and for having sent forces against it piecemeal. He called up from the south by radio, near the enemy's Phu Bon AO where they'd been picnicking, harrassing the lazy Mike forces, the nearest Chuck elements—three companies. He ordered them to travel north through the night on high-speed trails protected from sniffers by triple canopy. He ordered them to join Lieutenant Giap's makeshift company on the ridgeline, to sweep west to annihilate the

Yank guerillas, and to draw Brigadier General King's two paratroop companies into the valley where those three VC companies, and more the commander would send in the next day, could destroy the paratroops and the commander could bring out of their caves his antiaircraft guns to blow from the skies the five battalions King would surely send to their rescue.

The fight for Old Baldy would be repeated in the valley. Once again, at King's most frustrating moment, the commander would order the VC and NVA elements to disappear into the ground. If he could not beat general King and his limitless armies fed to him from across the sea, he could produce a very fine little battle—to humiliate King and to please his own higher—and a good body count. He was satisfied with that plan. First, however, he had to eliminate this dangerous Yank guerilla unit.

Giap had done the best he could with the men he had— had circled them before putting them to bed for the night. They were no better in the forest than were most Yankee units—uncomfortable, suspicious, clumsy, noisy—and they were unfit for a night operation against Bravo. He looked with growing respect at Captain Dong who had, after the horror of the eight-inch attack, pulled off his ragged clothes to his shorts, called six others—the only six unwounded VC—to do the same, daubed himself with mud and slithered off into the night heavily armed with rifles, knives, grenades, and three satchel charges brought by Giap's company. Dong's team moved south, the only logical direction in which Bravo might have disappeared, to hunt.

To the east of the moutain ridge which topped 170 meters at its highest peak, on a small, hastily fortified hilltop, the two commanders of the para companies huddled over a foxhole in which an RTO had raised Bravo Company on his radio. "Listen, Pagan-four," the RTO whispered into his handset, "if you hear me, break static twice, over." The two lieutenants huddled closer as the RTO held his handset away from his ear and raised the volume. *Click-click!* "We got 'em, sirs!" said the excited RTO.

"Yeah, and what do we do with 'em?" said First Lieutenant Cassidy to Second Lieutenant Pinch.

"We got a suggestion, sirs," said Pinch's field first sergeant accompanied by three more dirty, ragged, half-fought-out NCOs, their dull metal shotguns and grenade launchers black in their hands despite a wretched sliver of moon lighting too much of their FOB. The four NCOs squatted by the hole. "Pardon for sayin' it, sirs, but higher did us no favors puttin' us on this hill. Come morning, Chuck on those mountains over there can defillade us. If he's got rockets, mortars, or Winchesters, he's got us pinned here."

"We know that, Sarge. That's why we figure to call air support at dawn and move off this crest onto the ridgeline to meet Bravo at first light as they come over," said Pinch.

"Suggest, sirs, we move off a bit sooner, like now. We get ourselves up that ridge and into the trees in the dark, set up, dig in, and get ready for brother Chuck."

"My God, man!" said Cassidy. "You ever march in the dark?"

"On ambush, sir."

"That's a dozen guys. You're talkin about takin' one hundred-plus uphill through forest in the dark. Forget it." Cassidy gazed down at the notepad he held in his hand where the coordinates for various sniffer readings had been jotted. There were plenty of Chucks up on that ridgeline—forty, at least—but the sniffer had read nothing that could pass for Bravo, at least not at Bravo's reported laager. Bravo was well dug in or hidden below too-thick canopy to sniff.

The NCOs squatted stubbornly by the foxhole, unblinking, unmoving, waiting. Pinch rubbed the stubble on his chin and said, "Cassidy, why the hell you always say 'no' to a good idea first time you hear it and then 'yes' ten minutes later? Say 'yes' now and get it over with."

Said Cassidy, "I don't like this laager either, but Mad Mountain did pick it himself."

"Well, sirs," interrupted the field first sergeant, "it does our morale no good to be pulled off Old Baldy with fifty U.S. KIA and call it a draw. Now we're down here, the boys all been listenin' to Bravo's fightin' for four days, while we slogged up Old Baldy and didn't really hurt Chuck even though we took our hits, and now we're sittin' here like ducks once the sun's up and maybe what Chuck leaves us of these Bravos might be just enough to fill one body-bag?"

Cassidy looked over at Pinch and his jaw set; the stubborn man had made up his mind to take another stubborn road. "Whatdya say we give Chuckie a little technical warfare, Pinch? These sniffers are just thirty minutes old so we know what's out there but Chuck doesn't. What say we call for sniffers and redhaze every hour and use 'em for guidance as we climb the ridge? We call a little arty to keep Chuck awake and make the little bugger red-eyed in the mornin'. And when Bravo gets up the ridge, we're sittin' on top, dug in, ready to send out a couple of reinforced plats to lead 'em home. Eh?"

"A nice conservative approach," said Pinch. "Just what I woulda expected from you, Cassidy."

"I like it, too," said the stolid field first.

The first of Captain Dong's grenades went off on the western slope of the ridge, its report a muffled *bang!* "Yeah," said Pinch, scraping the itchy stubble on his jowl. "You," he said to Cassidy's RTO in the foxhole, "tell Bravo we're comin' up the hill and we'll meet 'em on the top at dawn. Get three clicks for reply. Let's go." The paras slipped off their hilltop and were gone as the sliver of moon sank beyond the earth, the Chuck observers in the hills around blinking in surprise at what they thought they had seen, but then discounting it—after all, Yanks never marched at night—and reporting nothing to higher. The watchers passed a safe and peaceful night watching an empty hill.

The grenade flung by Captain Dong bounced off the tree trunks and burst. Frags pricked and burned the GIs lying within fingertip reach in their circle, the brief yellow light of the burst showing Dong nothing—the Yanks were prone and well camouflaged. Nor did they open fire in reply. Good discipline, he thought, but he knew of no Yankee unit that could stand the battering he was going to give Bravo and not either run or fire into the two MGs Dong had brought from the NVA company. These Americans had a lot to answer for, not the least that excellently vicious trap they had set for Dong and Nguyen at the downed chopper, the trap that had made Dong see more clearly than at any other moment in the war that all the things he most loved but especially his soft, fat wife could be taken from him in an instant by impersonal, unexpected steel from some distant gun called on him by some equally coldhearted Yank hiding behind a tree. Dong would score some revenge kills tonight to hold Bravo here for the three Chuck companies humping up from Phu Bon, but most of all he would have the special satisfaction of murdering the men who had murdered his company.

He sent a man forward with a pistol wrapped in a piece of cloth to hide the flash, then sent two more slithering in the opposite direction to help determine the size and fortification of the enemy unit. He waited a half hour for them to get into place and to choose targets, then he hurled another grenade and, in its burst, the pistolman fired once and the others with rifles opened fire. There was a single prolonged agonized scream and no returning orange tracer fire from the Americans. The trick hadn't worked.

Dong lay unmoving for an hour, listening for sounds that would betray Yank movement, one of the three satchel charges in his hand. He was startled at the first distant burst of incoming artillery fire. Two rounds, Harrassment and Interdiction fire only, from the paratroopers on the other side of the ridgeline. He ignored it. During that hour, one of his men on the far side of the American laager hurled in another grenade and his men in two other locations fired bursts of automatic riflefire. But to none of that did the Yanks reply. Their fire discipline bordered on mania, thought Dong in frustration. He would have to stir them up with his satchel charge.

He began to crawl forward. There, jutting from a tree trunk at a ridiculous angle for a branch, was a long straight shadow. Dong wanted to cry out! It was a man standing there with a spear in his hand ready to pin him! The man fell forward, bloody foam spattering on the captain, the pungi spear driven through his chest still clutched in his hands with the blood-soaked, cloth-covered pistol. Dong rolled away from him and one orange tracer zipped into the earth by the dead man. Dong loosed at the enemy flash a green burst from his Ak47 and rolled away again. But there was no return fire.

He began to sweat, nervously wiping the jungle slime and salt sweat from his face. Another hideous scream! As though a big cat were clawing apart one of his men, and it *was* one of his men—he screamed for his mother in Vietnamese before his wail was choked off.

All right, thought Dong, I've lost two but I can't crawl back to an NVA company of clerks and cooks to tell them you frightened me away. He slithered forward, the satchel charge slung over his back, taking a long half hour to crawl twenty meters through the spongy jungle floor of vines, snakes, and startled little night creatures daring to skitter from their holes in the long silence since the screaming stopped. Far away and muffled through the jungle were the occasional bursts of harrassing artillery fire directed by the paratroops.

He heard at last the soft scrape of leaves on fabric as a

man wearing pants shifted position; he was within a body's length of the enemy line. Dong took long minutes to draw the satchel charge from his back, to put his hands on the fuze, to study the blackness around him looking for clues to his target. Ahead, he thought, and to the right. If he was close enough to hear a man shift his legs, he was close enough to throw the satchel into the very center of their position.

He glanced to his left and noted a thick tree root system rising from the base of a broad tree; that would give him all the protection from the charge that he would need. He studied it long minutes to be sure there was no one else in there among the roots, then he pulled the rasping fuze on the charge—the Americans had been waiting for him! The muzzle flashes of three rifles exploded in his face!—one round each rifle—good fire discipline—but he had hurled the satchel and was already rolling under the brush toward the thick roots—he heard the satchel strike the spongy earth in the enemy position and suddenly it erupted and there was screaming and bits of flying wood. He had rolled bumping into the huge root, trying to control his excited breathing so not go give himself away. He saw the Yank's face. The man half rose from his lair beneath the tree and with a single flash of blue metal slit the screaming Captain Dong from belly to throat.

Deerslayer rolled away, wiping on the earth the mess from his bowie knife, the screams of his buddies gradually muffled behind him.

A burst of green tracer spattered across Bravo's circle, their position defined by the satchel charge burst, and one impatient burst of orange replied, flinging the Chuck attacker into the forest.

Bravo's defensive circle shrank. They stripped the dead of weapons, ammo, water, food and left them where they lay. The wounded they shoved into the center of the circle as they edged backward until the circle of soldiers touching fingertips was again unbroken. It was now that the flyboy they had saved, the symbol of their triumph, with his broken wrists, groaned out of his sleep, and they realized that they had one more task to accomplish.

They roused him awake, the delirious survivor of the downed chopper, and he gawked at them unwilling to believe in them, frightened more of them than of Chuck. But the ghost soldiers came to him one at a time, Captain Daddy first, and touched him: Sar'n Mars and Waldo, Georgie Bee, Peepsite Taylor, Fruitcake, Pinball, Knobs, Deerslayer, Ayrab and the others. They said to him, Our part is almost done, buddy, but you have one more hike to make. In every battle of truth with falsehood, there is always one chosen to live to tell the tale. You are it. Tell them of us, tell America.

They lay through the last two hours of darkness, exhausted, trading clicks on the radio with the para companies coming up the mountain to meet them at first light. Their survivor lay conscious in the center of their circle, stunned by his new responsibility. This night for the Bravos there were no reveries of the war's end. The war would never end.

False dawn seeped into the jungle. Captain Foley, Waldo and Sar'n Mars moved crouching through their little FOB. They gazed upslope through the trees and yearned to be up on that ridge now with the para companies. They checked the chopper survivor to assure that he was well enough to march despite his broken wrists—he was infected, delirious yet silent. Bravo Company rose quietly from the seeping earth and slipped uphill through the trees, gathering what weapons they could from the corpses of Captain Dong and his men, delighted to find one of his two machine guns unharmed and two Ak47s, giving three clicks on their radio to the paras as warning.

The morning silence was oppressive. The distant *krump* of incoming arty fire directed by the paras was gone. Not a bird sang, not a brushbuck barked. There were no signs of slithering snakes or prints of cats to prove that any creature but Chuck had moved in the valley in that grim night. They marched in silence, using no machetes, slowed by the staggering pace of their wounded survivor and by their refusal to cut trail. They crouched uphill, staring round for Chuck, a weary, bloody, battered crew.

The forest thinned as they climbed; the triple-canopy disappeared. With the first full flash of morning, they looked up through the branches to see there on the slope above them a radiant splash of sun playing on the two companies of paratroopers swinging over the ridgetop coming down for *them!* There in the east, leaping up black and slick against the brassy morning sky, were six Cobras and a long stick of slicks. They were going to make it!

They burst through the trees running upslope—only one hundred meters to the paras—gasping and stumbling, and they charged into the startled faces of the three Chuck companies that had hastily set up on the ridgeline. A blaze of fire roared out of the enemy trees. Sar'n Mars shouted, "Charge the guns!" before his head exploded and Captain Foley was blasted flipping downslope into the trees. Bravo charged screaming into the enemy line—it would not be denied, Bravo had its survivor and its triumph—and Waldo and the Bee, yelling like lunatics, found themselves among the Chuck companies and shooting down the Chuck ambush line, the survivor running for the protection of the paratroops above them on the slope. The paratroopers shouted their battlecry and charged down into the Chuck rear. Gunships swooped down on the flanks chopping the Chuck companies, NVA Lieutenant Giap burst out of the trees leading his company of cooks and clerks in a flank attack, and Bravo disappeared before the eyes of the paratroopers and the gunnies, all the ghost soldiers vanishing, dead at last.

If you have enjoyed this book and would like to receive details of other Walker Adventure titles, please write to:

Adventure Editor
Walker and Company
720 Fifth Avenue
New York, NY 10019

Hardesty   007525331   c. 4
    Ghost soldiers.